This is all your FAULT, Cassie Parker

This is all your FAULT, Cassie Parker

TERRA ELAN McVOY

KATHERINE TEGEN BOOKS
An Imprint of HarperCollins Publishers

Katherine Tegen Books is an imprint of HarperCollins Publishers.

This Is All Your Fault, Cassie Parker
Copyright © 2016 by HarperCollins Publishers
All rights reserved. Printed in the United States of America.
No part of this book may be used or reproduced in any manner
whatsoever without written permission except in the case of brief
quotations embodied in critical articles and reviews. For information address
HarperCollins Children's Books, a division of HarperCollins Publishers,
195 Broadway, New York, NY 10007.
www.harpercollinschildrens.com

Library of Congress Control Number: 2015955195
ISBN 978-0-06-241449-6

16 17 18 19 20 PC/RRDH 10 9 8 7 6 5 4 3 2 1

First Edition

To everyone who's ever been a good friend to someone else.
but especially one to me

Chapter One

Cassie is positive we've been spotted, and slows down as though suddenly fascinated by the Hallway Etiquette poster over the water fountain. But this is the longest stretch we've ever walked undetected behind her crush, Cory Baxter (and the most conversation we've overheard between him and his friends), so I'm not letting her break this streak just because she's a little nervous. I tug a strand of her long, glossy black hair and make a "keep going" face without worrying whether or not she'll follow. I know she'll follow. Because Cassie loves the thrill of this game, too, and because she's more than a little obsessed with Cory.

She's back by my side in not even two steps, raising her eyebrows in silent "I can't believe this" excitement. We've been tracking Cory Baxter—code name: Lagoon—since we got back from spring break, when Cassie suddenly went googly-eyed in the cafeteria over him. Just like one of those old cartoons where someone gets hit in the chest by a Cupid arrow, or sniffs a love potion. It even caught *her* off guard.

But I'd had a similar feeling right before spring break myself, when Tyrick Nevin—code name: Pencil—and I were assigned to the same group for our vocabulary project. Tyrick had been in my English class all year, and was always thoughtful and quiet, but I had never considered him more than a nice classmate. Not until I was sitting across from him and realized that his eyes are a hypnotically golden color: light brown with a dark brown ring around the edge. I had never seen eyes such a color, and I found it hard to look at them and talk at the same time.

So I came up with a plan. Or rather, Cassie and I did, which is the way we always do things, ever since summer before fifth grade when we ended up in the same week of Girls Up camp and discovered the power of our collaborations. (For one: we are great at creating obstacle courses. Two: by harnessing my problem-solving skills and Cassie's competitive streak, we can get through everyone else's the fastest too.) There have been several more revelations like this since then, all demonstrating that we are meant to be best friends. She has good ideas—I have good ideas—but somehow when we share them we both get even better ones.

Like this Cory/Tyrick thing. My original thought was that we should learn as much about both of them as we could by observation—likes, dislikes, general interests—so that when we eventually talked to either one of them, we would have something clever and pertinent to say. This was admittedly easier for me, since Tyrick is in my class. All period I would take careful mental notes about the things he said, the way he tapped his pen on the desk when he was trying to come up with a word—whatever details I could grab on to—and then record them all in my diary. But Cassie didn't have as much luck, since Cory is an eighth grader. He has online accounts in the usual places, which was exciting to discover at first, but then we realized Cassie would have to follow him to see any of his posts, which would obliterate the secret element. Nobody really puts much in the school's web roster, so that wasn't any help, either.

Which is when she decided we needed to start spying on them both.

"This is it, this is it," Cassie whispers beside me, making sure to keep her lips from moving. We're rounding the corner from the long stretch of the research wing (where

Cory and his friends hang out before school) to the high-trafficked main corridor. This is when we change directions and weave our way through the crowd to the seventh grade hall, where, if there's time, we can catch a glimpse of Tyrick by his locker before the homeroom bell rings.

Now, rather than moving into the backpack-and-braces crowd toward our own hallway, Cassie links her arm through mine, hooking me tight. Her nervousness from a few minutes ago seems to have disappeared, and the determined expression on her face is the only cue I need. We plunge across the hallway traffic and keep following Cory and his friends into the eighth grade wing. As soon as we cross the threshold into the newer, smoother hall, we swap glances, reflecting to each other the same thrill: we've never gone this far before.

For the briefest moment, I'm disappointed I won't get an early peek at Pencil today—I like to know what he's wearing, in case it's one of the outfits he looks the best in, so I can prepare my face before I get to English class—but when Cassie gets that mischievous glint in her eye (the one that reminds me so much of her feisty grandmother, Tess), something fun is always going to follow.

Ahead of us, Cory waves bye to his friends—Jeannette (not his girlfriend, we were happy to discover), and Hopper (we don't know much about him other than he is Cory's favorite partner for some magic game that involves a lot of trading cards)—as they both enter the first classroom on our left. Now Cory is completely alone, and as far as we can tell, has no idea we're following him. Our arms are still linked, and Cassie squeezes mine between her jabby elbow and her rib cage. I can feel the vibrations of adrenaline rising in us both. There are still plenty of older kids out in the hall, so if Cory turned around he wouldn't exactly spot us, but the homeroom bell will be ringing in only a couple more minutes. We also have no idea where he's going, or how far.

But Cassie isn't slowing down, so I'm dying to see what she's going to do. From the way she's nibbling the edge of her lower lip, I can tell she is too.

Two doors farther, Cory ducks into his homeroom class: *Ms. Cruik, History*, the sign outside the door says. To my surprise and shock, Cassie follows him in, slipping her arm out from mine and sweeping her hair in one smooth, confident gesture over her shoulder. Cassie marches straight to Ms. Cruik's desk at the front of the room, and I have no choice but to follow, mainly because I have to hear what she's going to say.

It takes Ms. Cruik a moment to look up from her desk computer, but when she does, Cassie lights up her best, most teacher-charming smile.

"Hi, Ms. Cruik."

"It's 'cruck,' actually," the teacher says. "Like 'cluck' with an *r* instead of an *l*."

"Oh. Well, I'm sorry, Ms. Cruik"—she mimics the teacher's pronouncement perfectly, including the note of suspicion—"but learning more about upper-grade teachers is actually why we're here. My name's Cassie Parker, and my friend Fiona and I are having a hard time deciding which, um"—she glances at the whiteboard, obviously trying to remember what classroom we're in—"history class would be best for us next year. We know we don't have much control, but we'd like to know what to hope for."

Ms. Cruik is still doubtful, but she does straighten up a little.

"We're just wondering what you intend for students to gain by taking this class," Cassie continues.

Now Ms. Cruik's face transforms from distrustful to impressed.

"Well, Cassie, I'm happy to help. I hope that when they leave my class my students have a better understanding of the complex tapestry of American history, and become more intellectually enriched citizens because of it."

Cassie smiles. "Thank you, Ms. Cruik. Fiona, you've got that?"

"Um. Of course." I slide a notepad out of my book bag and dig for a pen. Over our heads, the homeroom bell chimes its ugly digital tone.

"Oh gosh," Cassie says, looking at the clock in mock horror. "I didn't realize we were going to be late. Ms. Cruik, I hate to impose, but do you mind giving us a pass? We have to get back to the seventh grade wing."

It's clear Ms. Cruik doesn't quite think our little poll is worthy of a hall pass. She glances at her still-chattering homeroom, though, and makes the decision that it's better to get us out of here and begin announcements rather than lecture us on time management.

The second her door shuts behind us, Cassie and I speed-walk down the now-empty eighth grade hallway, hands clamped over our mouths to keep our giggles from bursting out. The moment we're in the main hall, safely far away from Ms. Cruik's room or Cory's ears, we both jump up and down, squealing and talking over each other.

"I can't believe you did that!"

"I can't believe I just did that!"

"She had no idea you were faking."

"Do you think he was watching? I was too nervous to look around. But we were there! *In his homeroom class!*"

"You were so calm! I had no idea what you were going to say."

"I know! Me neither!"

We straighten and quiet down when one of the secretaries comes out of the staff bathroom farther down the hall. Both of us make sure to clutch our hall passes in clear sight as we start walking again.

"It's not a bad idea, though," I consider.

"What?"

"Polling more eighth grade teachers. I thought her answer was pretty good."

"Ugh." Cassie flicks her fingers in the air, dismissing it. "Her class sounds so boring. Besides, we already know whatever teachers Kendra Mack and Izzy Gathing sign up for next year are the ones we really want. And anyway, now we don't need to poll anybody else because we know Lagoon's homeroom!"

We're almost to our own homerooms ourselves, so I decide not to tell Cassie that I'm probably interested in the exact opposite classes that Kendra or her friends will be taking. For now, I don't want to ruin this fun.

"It still might be useful for future spy tactics," I say instead.

"True," she agrees. "Talk about it at lunch?"

I nod. She waves her pass at me with a sneaky wink, and I can't help grinning back.

Dear Diary:

What an up-and-down roller coaster of a day. I'm eager to slip into bed and get on my way to a new morning, but so much happened that I need to get it all straight in my head. Things started out fun this morning, with stalking Lagoon and <u>getting into his homeroom</u> (!!!). Cassie was brilliant as usual. It almost makes me sad that school's over soon and there'll be no more Pencil or Lagoon for a while, but at least we'll have the super-amazing Disneyland trip with Dad and Leelu to look forward to. (Which reminds me, Cassie and I need to look at the website and see what new rides there are since the last time both our families went.)

But anyway, then in third period—you won't believe it—<u>Pencil turned right around in his seat to talk to me before English class!</u> In that dreamy, Michael Bublé voice of his (extra low because he was trying not to be too loud, but still had to be heard over everyone getting out their books), he said, "Hey, Fiona. Are you okay?" My first instinct was to check my shirt to see if there were leftover breakfast bits on me, or if my arms had exploded in dripping pustules, but then he said, "I just didn't see you this morning like usual, so I wondered if you had an appointment." He wondered! If I had an appointment! <u>Because he didn't see me before school.</u> Which means he has been noticing me in the morning as much as I am noticing him!!! Diary, it was ten thousand vocabulary words at once: exalting, electrifying, astonishing, breathtaking, wondrous, and addictive. I could hardly concentrate on our out-loud reading in class, but when it got to my turn I read each word aiming my voice at the back of Pencil's head, hoping it might make him turn around again and look at me with those eyes.

So, of course I was dying to see Cassie at lunch, and when I told her my news, her mouth dropped open in a satisfyingly shocked smile. We bounced in our chairs about a zillion times—I'm surprised we didn't knock something over with how hard the table was vibrating.

But then her voice dropped and her expression changed. She said she needed good news, because her morning had been so depressing. I went straight into listening mode, thinking maybe it was about a grade, but instead she narrated this long thing about Neftali (in case you need a reminder: the prettiest one in Kendra's clan), some eighth grade boy named Carter, and him standing her up. Cassie seemed so serious about it, but by the time she finished, really it just sounded like Neftali misinterpreted some texts. When I asked her why she cared so much about a girl who didn't even know we existed, Cassie got that haughty, dismissive look on her face and muttered something about *how we could be as popular next year and she's just trying to do research. And get this, Diary—the way she found out the whole Neftali thing? She <u>followed</u> the two of them down the hall just like we do with Pencil and Lagoon! She said since it worked so well this morning, she wanted to try it again.*

Which—I have a lot to say about, including how disappointed I was that she used something of <u>ours</u> to get information about <u>them</u>. I knew, though, if I said anything else, *she'd give me the snotty silent treatment through science class, and I didn't want to ruin the good parts of the morning, but I just don't understand Cassie's fixation on those girls. Like the thing she said this morning about taking whatever classes they were signing up for. The last thing I want is to be anywhere near those spoiled show-offs. Yes, Cassie's always been interested in clothes and having a good reputation, but that's what I like about her—her emphasis on <u>good</u> reputation, not <u>popular</u> reputation. And she's never been so focused on her looks that she can barely think about anything else. At the end of lunch I swear she checked her lip gloss five times before we got up from the table. I tell you, I would rather listen to my uncles talking about yard work, watch* Frozen *with Leelu for the 7,321st time, do an entire worksheet of multiplying by fractions, or have to sit through an embarrassing* biology video more than talk about Neftali or Kendra. And definitely more than watching Cassie adjust her makeup.

We turned it around like we always do (on the way to science I asked her how our morning discoveries will change our spying, and she had lots to say about that), but it left a sour feeling in my heart.

Which (sorry for the long entry) made it even harder than usual to fake excitement when Jennifer came over again tonight. As if she hadn't already dominated this weekend, which, as you know, was supposed to be just us and Dad. She'd bought me and Leelu our own copy of Inside Out (the DVD has extra stuff on it you can't get from a download), and I admit it was super nice of her to remember how much Leelu and I loved it in the theater, but when it got to the part where the first island starts collapsing, instead of grabbing for my hand, Leelu crawled right up into Jennifer's lap. Jennifer slid her hand along the sofa cushions to try and hold mine as well, but I pretended I was too wrapped up in the movie to notice, mainly because some kind of island was crumbling inside of me at the same time. How could I hold hands with _her_? During a movie that's Leelu's and mine? Especially when we only met her four months ago? And suddenly my sister is all cuddly with her instead of me? I wanted to text Mom about it, but around the subject of Jennifer she stiffly says

Dad has every right to be happy. She's not the one who's getting this total stranger forced on her all the time, though. She doesn't have to pretend to be excited about a person she barely knows or likes, just because her dad (and now her sister) is all gaga.

It feels a lot better to tell you that, at least. Dad and Mom are so civil all the time, it's like I'm not allowed to have bad feelings. Luckily, I have Cassie, who's pretty much the only one who understands me. For now, thanks for being there, Diary. Hope it's a better report tomorrow.

Yours,
Fiona

Chapter Two

assie does help make things better in the morning. Before I've even washed my face, my phone is lit up with a bunch of emojis and Cassie's new plans for our stalking route. Now that we know Tyrick really is looking for me, she decides we need to start our morning patrol in our own hall, going first to her locker (because she has a mirror we can angle so that we spot Tyrick before he sees us) and then to mine (for which we have to walk past his), even if we don't need anything out of them.

Then to the library to stare at Lagoon, she messages.

Okay meet you at the bus drop-off, I tell her, hurrying down to get breakfast. Weeks when we stay at Mom's, she takes both Leelu and me to school, but at Dad's we have to ride the bus. It isn't the worst thing on the planet, but I don't think anyone in the history of middle school has ever enjoyed it.

Did things go okay last night? Cassie messages when I get to my bus stop.

Leelu likes Jennifer a lot more than I do, I admit.

Well she does bring you guys a lot of presents. Brainwashing, you know.

I smile a little at that. Cassie was the greatest friend ever last year when Mom and Dad told us they couldn't live together anymore. She helped me pack when Mom moved into the condo and we sold our house (Dad and Mom explained it would be better for Leelu and me to live somewhere that wasn't full of old memories), and helped me decorate my room in Dad's new place. If it hadn't been for her, Leelu, and the elaborate Nicholas Sparks–inspired story I wrote in my diary about my parents getting back together (even though they said it would never happen), I don't think I'd have survived. That Cassie isn't immediately trying to make me adore Jennifer like everyone else is exactly the kind of comforting that makes her the best friend in the whole world.

When she hops off her bus with a big smile, we hurry to catch a glimpse of Tyrick, and my bad feelings about last night fall to the background even further. Tyrick is in one of my favorite shirts, and gives me a one-handed "Hi" as we walk by. I'm not sure who's bouncing more on the way to the library, where we'll spy on Lagoon: me or Cassie.

"You're so gonna get asked out before the end of the year," she hisses when we find a table and settle in.

I feel myself flush.

"I wonder if we could double with—oh. Six o'clock." She ducks her head and leans close to the desk, having spotted someone interesting behind me—someone other than Cory, who we already know is in the computer lab, thanks to earlier scopes, and the wall of windows between it and the library. Whoever Cassie's spotted now could have on a great outfit, or be picking their nose—it's hard to tell from her expression.

Before I can get a glance, though, my chorus friend Evie comes in with her best friend, Aja. They see us and wave, coming over to our table.

"Are you guys studying?" Evie rushes in a loud whisper. "We didn't know you hung out here. Can we study with you too? We have that math test coming up and—ooh, Fiona, I love your hair that way."

Automatically, I reach up to feel my head, making sure everything is still lying down flat. For most of the year, my hair's been a kinked-out curly crown that sproings up all around my face and ears, unlike Evie's, which she gets done into glossy spirals. I've been growing mine out, just to experiment, and now it's finally long enough to wear in a bun-looking pony if I sleek it all down tight with tons of product, lots of brushing, and what feels like a hundred bobby pins jammed into the sides. I'm constantly expecting it to turn a bit flyaway, though, and sometimes wonder if I shouldn't just cut it back.

"Huh?" Cassie snorts, her whole face tightening with criticism. "Just because Fee's got fluffiness doesn't mean she can't be sleek, too. I mean, is that such a surprise?"

It stuns me, and Evie too.

"Of course I love it natural," Evie stammers, "but this is so . . . sophisticated." She darts her eyes at me in apology.

But before I can say or do anything, Aja leans on the table with one hand, putting her body between Cassie and Evie. A wave of her spicy perfume wafts over us.

"Do you think you'll keep growing it?" she asks, as if my hair is suddenly the most interesting topic of conversation.

Aja is a tall, Egyptian-queen-looking girl, and while we know each other because of Evie and chorus, we don't normally hang out. She's perfectly nice, but somehow her closeness now is intimidating, especially since Cassie was just so horribly rude. I say something clumsy about somewhere between my chin and my shoulders, though with summer just about upon us, I might get hot.

Cassie hasn't even noticed. Her focus is back to the glass windows. Behind them in the lab, Cory must be getting ready to make his move to homeroom, because Cassie starts getting her things together so we can follow him. We can't go in there because without a coding project (only for eighth graders) we'll look too obvious, but from here we can see perfectly. Right now, I'm just glad to have a way out of this situation.

"I'll see you in chorus, okay?" I apologize to Evie and Aja with my face.

"Have a good first period," Evie chirps behind us, like everything is fine.

As we stride out of the library, Cassie super-widens her eyes so that she looks like a silly manga character, mouthing, *Have a good first period.*

Again, it's shocking.

"Hey, did something happen with Tom yesterday?" I say, careful.

She looks surprised. "No, why? Did he post something about me?"

"No. I mean, if he did, I wouldn't know. You just seem on edge today."

Mean is the word I want to use, but I need to be cautious. Cassie and her brother, Tom, have been fighting more than usual lately—or, more specifically, she's been fighting with her parents about her brother, who's older and in their eyes perfect—and sometimes it leaves her pouty and sensitive. If I'm not careful her temper will flare up from nowhere at me, and *we'll* end up in a fight.

She rolls her eyes. "Ugh. I know you like her and everything, but sometimes that Evie can be, you know."

"Can be what?" I like Evie. She's nice.

Cassie makes another sickeningly sweet face—with the emphasis on sick. "A little too much is all. She should have learned to tone down the sunshine by now. We're not in sixth grade anymore. She doesn't have to be everyone's friend."

"Well, she's my friend," I say.

She tosses me a humble shrug. "I'm glad she likes you so much, I guess," she says. "And your hair does look sophisticated that way."

It's still not much of a peace offering, but I understand it's the closest thing to an apology as I'll get right now.

"We'll see if it holds up by lunch." I smooth my hair a bit more, deciding to let the issue go. "And whether Pencil has anything to say about it."

With that, she squeaks in excitement, and we follow Cory once again into the eighth grade wing. We don't go all the way to his homeroom this time, because we can't be late again, but Cassie's thrilled anyway. I'm just glad she's happy, though when we separate for homeroom she hollers "Ciao, bella!" at me the way Kendra and all her other friends do. In a way that sounds practiced.

I can't believe it's already a mixed-up morning, or that I need my diary so soon, even for just a quick entry.

Ebullient girl
Vivacious and sweet
Interested in everyone
Even if some think it's too much.

Amazon queen
Just waiting to pounce
And silence you with her kohl-eyed stare.

Catty without cause
Always
Silently judging
So confident in her opinions
Immune to
Everyone else's.

It feels like a mean thing to write about my best friend, but also good to get down, because I don't want to dwell on negative feelings about Cassie. I decide to turn things around when I see her again at lunch.

"We need to make a list," I tell her when we get to our table.

She grins, sly. "Ways to sabotage your dad's romance?"

"Ha. Maybe tomorrow. This, you may be surprised to hear, is more important." I show her the fresh, blank page in my notebook, across the top of which I've written *PLANS FOR DISNEYLAND*.

Cassie fake swoons against her chair. "Finally my dream of freeing Aladdin from my evil twin, Jasmine, is within reach!"

"You might want to explain that little third grade infatuation to Lagoon first." I nod over at their table. We have a perfect view from here, but they can't quite see us.

"Oh, I don't know. Maybe we need a vintage Disney marathon this weekend, so I can get her moves down. I may have forgotten the best ones."

"Hopefully Jennifer won't butt in this time," I grumble.

But Cassie's not going to let me go down that path today. She pulls me up to get in line for our drinks, humming "A Whole New World" close to my ear, and doesn't even acknowledge Kendra's gang when we pass their table, or seem to care about Cory, either. When we're through the line, she does a little Wizard of Oz–style skip to our seats, and takes out her best pen to write down all our ideas: the rides we'll have to do multiple times, the ones Leelu's finally big enough to go on with us, the food we want to try, plus the shows at night we can't miss.

"And Haunted Mansion at least five times," she insists.

I cross my eyes and make my face like a cartoon ghost's. "Of course!"

As the list builds, we feed off each other's excitement, both of us getting giddier and sillier. By the time lunch is over and we're walking to science, we're positively hyper—Cassie squeaking in a Minnie Mouse voice—neither of us caring who sees or overhears, just like in fifth grade.

It isn't until we get to class when I stop. "Oh no."

Cassie sees my face and halts, too. "What is it?"

"My backpack."

Her expression immediately becomes serious. "Let's go look."

We speed-walk back to the cafeteria, Cassie assuring me the whole way my bag's surely still under my chair right where I left it. I want to believe her, but I can't help thinking of the video Dad made me watch when I got my cell phone, about how important it is to keep your eyes on your things, because somebody could snatch them at any time.

But of course Cassie's right—my backpack's still in the cafeteria. Only, now it's shoved under a chair two tables away from where we sit. We trade worried glances.

"Just noticed it myself," Mr. Olansky, the lunchtime supervisor, says. "Was going to finish locking up, and then look for an ID."

I thank him and check inside, trying not to panic. In the small front pocket are my house keys, and my money purse—nothing missing from that, including my library card, which may not matter to anyone else, but matters a lot to me. My phone is still in the elastic-edged inner pocket too, and nobody would want my pen case, since it was a gift from Leelu and therefore is covered with pictures of Doc McStuffins. The main section of my backpack—the one with my tablet, my notebooks, my books and other binders—still gapes open. But everything's there too, except—

"What is it?" Cassie says, seeing my face.

My stomach detaches from my body. "My diary, Cassie. I think it's gone."

Chapter Three

M r. Olansky lets Cassie and me search for my diary under all the cafeteria tables, and even offers to look through the trash for it. I want to cry, picturing the cover's beautiful marbled Italian paper stained with pizza sauce, or its pages soaked with half-drunk milkshake, but if it's in the trash at least I'd know my secrets were safe, instead of being pored over by whoever might have taken it.

"You have to get back to class," I tell Cassie, trying to be rational.

"And you should get a pass to keep looking."

I tell Mr. Olansky I'll be back, before Cassie and I walk in glum silence together to science. It's good Cassie knows not to try and make me feel better, because I'm not sure anything can make me feel better right now. My diary is like my best friend—more than my best friend, since I write things in there I would never even say to Cassie. It's where I've poured out absolutely everything, no matter how angry or ugly or embarrassing, including— my body prickles with horrified heat—all those details about Tyrick.

When we get back to science, I tell myself not to freak out, that I'll surely find it, and ask Ms. Tasker for a pass to go back to the cafeteria. Luckily, she is not only brilliant but also very, very nice, and she writes me one without hesitation. When I return to the lunchroom, Mr. Olansky has already gone through one of the three bulging trash cans with no luck, but he tells me he's had to do this many, many times, for lost retainers or phones, and hands me a pair of latex gloves.

Picking through people's half-eaten sandwiches, soggy hot lunches, and discarded pizza crusts is gross, but at least it gives me something to focus on, until we get through the last bag and my desperate hope of finding my diary is dashed and ruined.

"I'm sorry, kiddo." Mr. Olansky pulls off his gloves and tosses them into the last bag. "Most of the time, we find what we're looking for."

I thank him and throw away my own gloves, trying hard as I can to steel my face until I can be alone. So many horrible thoughts are swirling in my brain about who might have my diary now, or what they might do with it, I'm not sure I can breathe. Thank goodness there are bathrooms right outside the lunchroom doors. I slip inside, rush to the last stall in the row, lean against the wall, and cry.

I don't say anything to Cassie after science, because we both know neither of us can say anything that will make a difference. She lets me slip down the hall without more than a wave, and for my final periods I try to make my mind as blank as possible. At the last bell, though, Cassie's somehow gotten out of her own class early and is waiting outside the chorus room for me. I'm surprised, but also relieved, and when Aja and Evie pass us and wave goodbye, I can even manage a small, genuine smile.

"I thought I'd walk you to the pickup," Cassie says.

"But you'll miss your bus."

She shrugs. "You might need company. I'll call my dad."

"Then you'll have to wait for him, silly. We could give you a ride if Leelu didn't have dance."

Cassie winces in sympathy. Leelu's dance means I have to do my homework perched on a folding chair in the corner. "Are you sure you're okay?"

"Go ahead." I'm not exactly sure I will be okay, especially if I don't have my diary to write in about how awful today has been, but there isn't anything Cassie can do. "I should probably study for math. And I can always read."

"You've got *Little Women*? For comfort?"

I pat my backpack. "At least they didn't take that."

We're at the top of the hall, where she needs to head right and I need to head left, but Cassie hesitates again, giving me a sympathetic look.

"Really, it's okay."

She's still worried. "Call me later?"

I nod. She squeezes my hand, and clearly doesn't want to leave, but she really needs to catch her bus.

"Sissie, you take forever," Leelu groans when I hop into the back of our nanny Maritza's car with her.

"Shut up," I tell her, fierce.

"Maritza!" she hollers, startled just as much as I am by my own ugly tone.

"Both of you, quiet." Maritza's voice is tense. While she drives a giant Suburban, and has been in Monterey since she moved from her tiny Texas town six years ago, traffic still makes her nervous. "Fiona, you know about that kind of language."

Instead of answering either of them I take out my phone

and text Mom: **Something bad happened in school today.**

So sorry to hear that, she types immediately back. **I'm just getting out of a meeting, and have some things to wrap up before I meet Rachel for dinner. Do you want to talk on the phone before bed?**

I guess, I tell her.

You are a beautiful rose surrounded by carnations, she says, trying to make me feel better. But right now all I feel like is a bramble of twisted thorns and weeds.

Trying to study during Leelu's dance practice doesn't help. It's difficult to memorize anything with Leelu and her friends floating around the studio to Jason Mraz anyway, but especially with all the horrible questions swirling in my mind about my diary. Who has it? Why did they take that instead of something else, and what are they going to do with it? Do they even know who I am? Did they do this on purpose? And if so, why? Out of panic and fear I check the school message board and all my feeds about a hundred times, waiting to see if whoever did this might be bragging about having my diary, or even posting passages there, but nothing shows up. I text Cassie too, hoping that she'll quell my mounting fears, but her battery must be dead again because she never texts back.

At dinner (salads picked up on Dad's way home, but at least we're eating together at our own dining room table, and there's no Jennifer this time) Dad asks us how our days were.

Before I can say anything, Leelu says, "Fiona's in a bad mood."

"Is that right?"

Normally it's nice that my little sister knows my moods so well, and wants me to feel better, but there's no way I can talk to Dad about this right now, especially since I'm not really sure how bad it all is yet.

"Just school stuff," I say.

"Is anyone giving you any trouble?" he wants to know.

I shake my head. *Not yet anyway.* If I tell Dad what really happened, he'll just give me a disappointed lecture about keeping better track of my things. And then he'll probably insist on coming to school so we can report my missing diary to the principal and the school security officers. Dad could have them do a search of everyone in the entire school if he wanted to, and that would only make things worse than they already are. Nobody would ever forget a mandatory locker search for something like a diary. Probably I'd still get teased about it at my high school graduation.

"Well, if things don't improve after a good night's sleep and another try at it tomorrow, I hope you'll let us know."

I mumble something that could be interpreted as a yes, and excuse myself to my room. In my desk drawer are three more journals people have given me for my birthday or Christmas, since everyone in my family knows I like to write, but I don't want any of those diaries—I want *my* diary: its soft, blue-swirled-with-lavender cover and perfect-thickness paper. And I want my mom not to be out with a friend so she can make me feel better. Most especially, I want Cassie to call me back. I've tried three times since school got out, but she's still not answering, and I need her to help me troll the internet and make sure no one's broadcast my most private thoughts all over everywhere. But after looking at the same sites alone over and over, there isn't anything to do but try to study. Still, before I go over my notes, I flip to a random blank page in my plain notebook for English, date it, and write two single words:

    Today sucks.

The first thing I hear when I step off the bus the next morning is a high-pitched voice squeaking, "Oh, Fiona, there you are!"

My diary anxiety made it hard to get to sleep last night, and when I finally did, I had strange, shadowy dreams of being lost in a giant concrete maze. Evie has to grab my arm before I realize it's her talking to me.

Her eyes search my face. "Are you okay? I heard what happened. I'm sure it isn't as bad as it sounds. Everyone knows Izzy always has to exaggerate everything."

The mention of Kendra's best friend and head minion makes everything jerk to attention. "Izzy?"

Evie's face shifts from worried and shocked, to embarrassed and uncertain. "You mean Cassie didn't tell you?"

"Didn't tell me what?"

Her mouth twists to the side. "Didn't tell you what happened yesterday, with your diary. It wasn't really Izzy, anyway. More like . . ."

She doesn't want to say it, and I don't need her to. The apologetic agony in her eyes as we move into the hall makes it plain: *more like Kendra Mack.*

Immediately I want to sink against the wall, and huddle in a moaning, humiliated heap. If Evie already knows about my diary this early in the morning, then it means pretty much everyone in the entire seventh grade could, possibly more. But if Kendra and Izzy really have my diary, the last thing I need is someone catching me bawling in some video on their phone.

"I heard it from Blake," Evie explains. "She told me Jordan was on the bus with them when it happened. Kendra had your diary and she and Gates were . . . they were messing around."

Her vagueness only makes me panic more. "What did they do?"

"Well, you know what a show-off Kendra is." Evie tries to downplay. "Always so dramatic."

"And?" I demand, picturing Kendra and Gates pitching my diary all over the bus, batting it to everyone on board. When she hesitates, I put my hand on her arm. It is thin and cool and the exact color of dried-out pine needles. "Evie, the homeroom bell's about to ring, and I need to know what I'm walking into."

She looks at the ceiling as though the words will be written there for her. "She was reading parts of it out loud."

Something takes over me, and I start walking down the hall, fast. Evie's calling out, but I'm already a span of lockers away from her.

"I'm fine." I wave behind me. I think I even smile. "I'll talk to you more in chorus, okay?"

My feet are walking one-two-one-two fast and hard, though I'm not sure where to yet. Because if Kendra has really read my diary out loud on the bus, there's absolutely nowhere I can hide.

In homeroom I go straight to my desk and sit down, not looking at anyone but not not-looking, either. There's no way to know who exactly has heard about this, or what parts of my diary got read aloud. Everyone in this room could know my secrets, and I want to dissolve. First, there's all the sad and miserable stuff I wrote during the Divorce, which would be embarrassing just because it's so pathetic, but what's much, much worse is everything about my crush on Tyrick. Every tiny thing he's said, what he's worn, how his voice makes me feel like I'm listening to one of Dad's playlists full of old crooners. I try to take deep breaths, tell myself maybe only a few people on Kendra's bus know, plus Evie and her friend. It probably isn't as bad as I can imagine.

But even if only a few people know, *Cassie* rides the same bus as Kendra Mack. She was most definitely there when this happened. So why didn't she warn me last night? Even if her own phone battery was dead (which happens all the time), she could've used Tom's, or her mom's, or else emailed me at least. She can't have thought it would be better to tell me in the morning. And if there was some bizarre reason why she lost all ability to communicate, how come she wasn't there waiting for me when I got off the bus? Why did it have to be Evie who found me first?

And how did Cassie let any of this happen to begin with?

I slip out a pen and a piece of paper while Mr. Jackson calls roll to write a note to drop in Cassie's locker first thing. Probably she has a reason for all of this, but if I'm going to make it through this nightmare, I need to hear it from her right away, so that we can figure out what to do. I'm confused, and upset, and trying not to feel mad, so it's hard to decide how to start. As I'm considering the right words, Isabella in the desk behind me taps me on the shoulder.

"Hey, Fiona," she whispers, trying to sound serious but failing. "I saw you writing some more secrets, and I thought you might want to use this." She giggles, and so do a couple of other kids around us, because she's holding out a pencil.

I glare at her and crumple up my note to Cassie. Why she didn't tell me isn't so important; I just need my best friend to help me deal with all this, and fast.

Isabella's not the only one with the mortifying pencil idea. Between homeroom and third period, at least twenty people ask me if I need to borrow one, or pass one across the room, to put on my desk. As soon as I sit down in English, somebody tosses one against the back of my head, which is even more crushingly awful because I can't stand up for myself. If I did, Tyrick would definitely turn around to see what's going on. All I can do, the entire class, is write over and over in my English notebook, *Please don't let him know. Please don't let him know. Please please please don't let him know, and if he doesn't yet, please don't let him find out.* Since

I recorded so many careful notes about him in my diary, it wouldn't take a whole lot more reading for somebody to figure out who Pencil really is. The idea of Kendra discovering my crush is bad enough, but if Tyrick heard even a fraction of what I wrote about him since spring break, I'd have to change schools.

Luckily, I make it to fourth period with at least that secret intact, if not my pride. The second I walk into class, though, Sage Hayden, who sits up front and is always making nasty jokes, says, "Hey, Fiona, I know a better name for your secret lover boy that starts with a *p*, too. It ends with an *s* and rhymes with—"

His friend hits him on the back of the head before he finishes, but I know the gross word he means. They both start laughing, and I do my best to ignore them—and the three girls who try to hand me pencils as I walk to my seat.

When I sit, Edgar McCutchins slips a note on the side of my desk before I even get my bag set down. I don't want to see, hear, or read one more mean or snarky thing today or ever, but Edgar hasn't folded his paper well and part of it gaps open. I catch only a couple of words: *apologize*, and *a question*.

Edgar is quiet, and a little smelly, and doesn't have enough friends to be mean to much of anyone, so I go ahead and read the whole thing.

Excuse me Fiona, but I want to apologize for the way you've been treated, and also ask you a question. I'm sorry someone took your diary from you, but I couldn't help overhearing about it, and your anonymous crush. I was just wondering if it might be me? I would be flattered, wouldn't tell anyone, and would of course say yes.

I blush so hard, there's no way my skin's dark enough to keep people from seeing. All I need on top of everything else today is people thinking I like someone as awkward and hygienically challenged as Edgar.

Thank you, Edgar, I write back on a clean sheet of paper, so that I can destroy the note he gave me. *But absolutely not.* I underline *not* four times, give it three exclamation points, and hand it back to him, before putting my head down on my desk and wishing I could suddenly transform into the kind of kid who sleeps through class, just to make time go faster until it's lunch, where at least I can find an answer— and a solution—from Cassie.

Chapter Four

bolt so fast out of my desk at the end of math that I nearly take it with me. I still need to get my science books for after lunch, but I skip my locker and go straight to the cafeteria, so I can sit down at our table before too many other people get in there. Including and most especially Kendra.

I take out my favorite book, *Little Women*, and pretend to read, but secretly I'm watching every person who comes through the door, feeling dashed and disappointed each time it's not the familiar face of my best friend, even if she may be a lousy one right now. At the first glance of Kendra's long curly red hair I sink as low in my chair as I can, praying the fiercest prayer I've ever prayed that she will not come over here and say something to me in front of the entire cafeteria.

But she doesn't even glance my way. Instead she chatters with Cheyenne as the two of them glide over to their table at the front of the lunchroom. Izzy and Neftali follow behind without looking around either, as though this is just another normal day for them. After a few minutes, they all jump out of their seats, but it's only to wave Gates and Billy over, like they haven't seen them all day.

After a few tense moments of waiting to see if one of them will head my way, I finally let go of the death grip I've had on my book. It loosens even further when Cassie finally jerks open the cafeteria door, although the look on her face (part worried, part resigned, and part—mad?) gives me pause. Probably my own face is doing similar things though, so when our eyes connect mostly I feel relieved. She's seen me, she's coming, and I know even if we have to have a difficult conversation about what happened, we're going to figure it out.

Which is when Kendra and her big, pink, lipsticked mouth shouts out, "Hey, Cassie Parker—where you going?" Like Cassie's supposed to have been sitting with them the whole time.

At first Cassie glances around as though this is a trick (which is what I think too), but then everything goes into slow motion as she pauses and takes a longer look at Kendra's table. She keeps walking one or two more steps toward me, and I think she's decided to ignore them, but then her eyes change and she gets this strange blank look on her face, before reassembling it into a smile, squaring her shoulders, and turning

back

around

to sit with them.

I'm so stunned, I think maybe my heart has stopped. I tell myself she's walking over there just to give Kendra the piece of mind she should have yesterday, but no. Cheyenne scoots over to make room while Izzy grabs an empty chair from the next table, and Cassie happily settles in with the same girls who stole my diary and read it out loud. The ones who laughed at me, and made my private thoughts a joke for our entire grade. She is sitting with them and she is looking satisfied with herself, and I wish a hole would open up in the ground and swallow me right there.

"Is this seat taken?" a voice says over me.

It's Edgar. Who is apparently ignoring my message from math.

"Um, I—" I look down the table to Yel, Daria, and their other basketball teammates for help, but there are at least four empty seats between them and me, and we're not friends anyway. "I have to do some reading," I say lamely. Edgar doesn't need to know I've already read *Little Women* three times.

"All right," Edgar says, and then sits down anyway. So there's nothing left for me but to try to find comfort in Marmee, Jo, and the March girls, while Edgar eats in silence, his mildewy-laundry smell filling the space between us.

When the bell finally rings, though, I remember my next class is science—with Cassie. I take my time putting my uneaten lunch carefully back into my bag, hoping maybe she'll come over from Kendra's table and explain all of this, but she walks right out with them and doesn't look my way. The cafeteria clears out around me, but I stay sitting there, shocked and numb.

"You find your book?" Mr. Olansky is pushing in chairs at the table next to mine.

"Pardon?"

He points to the trash cans. "You know. Yesterday? Hey, you feeling all right? Looks like you might need the clinic."

There's nothing Ms. Desir can offer me in the clinic to make me feel better about any of this, but at least there I won't have to face Cassie in science. I nod weakly, and let Mr. Olansky walk me down the hall, carrying my backpack for me the whole way.

· · ·

I don't have to fake feeling sick to my stomach, so Ms. Desir lets me stretch out on a cot and put a damp cloth over my eyes through fifth period. As I lie there in the cool white room, I replay the last few days in my head over and over, trying to think of anything I might have done or said that would make Cassie act like this. We've had such a fun week, at least in my mind. She was super excited about Disneyland yesterday and she was so sweet to meet me at the end of school. Was I not thankful enough? In my worry, was there some distressed comment she made that I missed?

Or is this some elaborate plan of Cassie's to get back at Kendra for taking my diary in the first place? Is she spying on them, looking for the best kind of revenge? It still doesn't make sense why she couldn't have told me about it, especially now that it's clear they read stuff out loud about *Pencil*, but maybe she has her reasons? To make it seem more real?

I just wish I knew what she knew. What else, what else did they read yesterday? Was it just the Pencil nickname thing? Or did she recite one of those embarrassing sonnets I wrote with all the vocabulary words from our project— the one we were assigned to together that made me start liking him in the first place?

My head swims with this through sixth period, which Ms. Desir lets me keep lying down for too, but I know I can't get out of my final class. I have to get to chorus, and I have to hear from Evie what more she might know.

"Fiona, are you okay?" Evie asks me right away.

I shrug, not sure how to answer.

"Just that—I heard—you know, Cassie. And lunch today. Jane told me that she was sitting with Kendra Mack."

"Evie, what else did Blake tell you? About what Kendra read on the bus."

"I don't think it was that much."

"Besides the—" I stop as a couple of altos come up and get their music folders. They walk away, giggling, and I drop my voice to an even lower whisper. "Besides the pencil thing, was there anything else? Anything specific?"

I can tell Evie feels torn. "Kendra was mad you said something about her in there, I think. And Gates is passing around some poll. About boyfriend nicknames."

A horrible thought occurs to me: that Kendra might've read something about Lagoon, too. How Cassie and I started watching *Doctor Who* in an attempt to understand Cory and his friends better. That Cassie has been playing more video games with Tom.

"Was there anything else, Evie? You have to think. Anything, maybe, about Cassie?"

Aja comes in right then, startling both of us. "That Cassie is a big fake," she says, dropping her handwoven shoulder bag among the rest of the backpacks. "Fiona's way better off." When she holds up her hand for me to high-five, bangles slide and clink down to her elbow, and her dark gaze is fixed on my less-sure one. "Can't abide the haters, Fee. Gotta shake little flies like that right off."

She hooks her arm around my shoulder and walks with me and Evie to our section before joining the rest of the altos. While I can't high-five anyone over what's happened, and this new nightmare that Kendra might've read something about Cory—or worse, Cassie—maybe having someone like Aja suddenly on my side could make things a tiny bit less terrible.

At the end of school I fast-track it to the pickup loop without speaking to or looking at anyone. The second I get into the car, Maritza offers to take me and Leelu out for frozen yogurt, somehow knowing right away I've had another bad day. Once I register what she's said, I see Leelu's poor little cheeks are streaked with tears. It helps me switch at least momentarily from Humiliated Outcast to Strong Big

Sister. Ever since the Divorce, Leelu's had these temper tantrums, sometimes over the littlest things, and she's needed a lot more help from me to get through them. Mom says it's because she's sad and angry about her family getting split up but doesn't know how to say it in clear ways, and that we need to be more patient with her. The truth is, though, comforting Leelu has comforted me a lot in the last year, too.

While we wait in line at the yogurt machines, I keep Leelu close, and listen while she pouts out something about not being picked for tetherball in PE today. It pales in comparison to my own middle school horrors, but I hum the chorus of Leelu's old favorite, "Let It Go," anyway, hoping we can both channel a little Elsa toughness.

But Leelu's scowl only deepens. "Stop making fun of me," she growls, heaping way too many Oreo crumbles on her yogurt.

"I'm not making fun of you." I gently take the spoon from her. "Tell me what's so bad about having to do tumbling with everyone else instead."

Her brows pull even closer together. "On the mats everyone can see your underwear."

Maritza tries not to laugh as she pays for our yogurt. "Not if you're wearing pants, silly."

Leelu's eyes widen in earnest. "Uh-huh. Simone had on

leggings and a long shirt and you could still see the band when she did her somersaults. Everyone was laughing because there were purple elephants on it."

"Well, that wasn't very nice of them," Maritza says when we sit down. "She was only enjoying herself and her exercise. There isn't anything to make fun of about that. Besides, elephants are majestic, and purple is the color of royalty."

Leelu's not convinced. "I still don't like tumbling. What if it happens to me?"

"There are worse things than being laughed at," I say, although I know better than she thinks how bad it does feel. "Maritza's right, it isn't nice, but"—I think of Aja—"you can find friends who won't think it's funny. They'll take your side and help you feel better."

I pull my chair closer to Leelu, so our knees are touching and I can lean forward to press my forehead against hers. "We'll make sure every morning that your underpants aren't showing too, okay?"

She shuts her eyes, still sad.

Maybe we both need something to look forward to. "What if we have a slumber party this weekend, huh? Will that take your mind off things?"

She keeps her eyes closed but nods just slightly enough for me to feel it.

I sit back up. "Hey, Maritza?"

"Yes, my sweet."

"Would it be okay if I invited friends over on Friday? For a slumber party?"

"We'll check with your father, but with me it is all right. I'm assuming they will come directly after school?"

"If that's okay?"

Leelu sits up straighter too. "Can we play TVD?"

TVD stands for "True Voice Dancing"—a game she made up involving our old karaoke machine, a judge's panel, dress-up clothes, and what she calls ballroom dancing, but is really just gliding around Dad's polished stone floors in socks.

"If they want to," I say. Aja would probably be good at TVD, actually, if she doesn't think it's too little-girlish.

"How many?" Maritza asks.

"Just two."

"I will speak to your father and then we will see."

"We can make brownies." Leelu perks up even more. "Or brownie sundaes."

I scrape another curl of yogurt with the edge of my spoon, warming up to the idea of kicking off Memorial Day weekend with ice cream, games, movies, and whatever else my friends might want to do, cheering up Leelu and myself at the same time.

46

But I've never had my chorus girlfriends over for a spend-the-night, because usually if anyone was coming over before, it'd be Cassie. Thinking of not seeing her through the whole long weekend drives me to take out my phone, see if she's sent me a message, but the screen is blank. It makes me even more desperate to hear from her, but right now I don't know what to say. If it's true that Kendra read some of the bad things I wrote about her group, maybe she also read how I felt about Cassie liking them.

A cold feeling crawls over me that has nothing to do with the frozen yogurt. I'd deserve it if Cassie was mad at me for that. Probably a long weekend apart will help us both get over it and make up, but in the meantime I think I could use whatever support I can get.

Chapter Five

Though Dad says okay to the slumber party, and Mom says, during our quick before-bed call, that she's glad I'm branching out to some new friends, I still can't get Cassie, my diary, or all the possible hideous scenarios I'm imagining out of my head. Living Cassie-free the next morning isn't so easy, either. During breakfast while I check my feed, there's a photo Cassie's posted of her smiling big with Cheyenne and Neftali. My first impulse is to block her, so I don't have to see anything else, until I remember my earlier thought that this could all be some double cross on Cassie's part. Maybe through these photos she'll send me a signal. I try to cling to it as I get ready to leave, even though the possibility of that feels less likely with every hour I don't hear from her.

Looking at the picture another five times on the bus only makes me know for sure I'm lying to myself that Cassie's doing this for my benefit. She's probably in pig heaven. And since Cassie's so tight with Kendra now, they probably showed her my entire diary. Which means even if Kendra didn't read anything negative about Cassie on the bus before, by now she will have seen every mean sentence I ever wrote, without a chance to explain. Probably she's helping them come up with an even better way to make my life miserable. I spend the rest of the bus ride combing Cassie's feed, plus Kendra's (and then Izzy's), searching for the tiniest hint that they've posted any quotes from my diary, or are concocting some terrible plan. Though most of their messages are full of hearts and emojis and exclamation points, they could still all be texting passages to everyone they know. Today could be even worse than yesterday, and I still don't have my diary to write things out.

Which means I just have to think of a way to get it, and my best friend, back.

When I step off the bus, I know better than to wait for Cassie to arrive, but I'm not sure where to go, either. Presumably Kendra will whisk her off to the courtyards, but should I walk our regular route, just in case? Or try to find Evie and Aja?

I trudge to my locker, to at least get a glimpse of Tyrick and see if, after yesterday, he suspects anything about my crush. Maybe I'll spot Cassie, too.

But after six minutes of cleaning old crumpled papers out of my locker, and rearranging things inside (plus sixty-five different furtive glances down in Tyrick's direction, even though I can't fully see him), I know I'm looking foolish. It isn't helping me get my diary back, either. I shut the door with a hard slam, not sure where to go next. The library? To keep spying on Lagoon? Will Cassie miss that, or have her new pals already given her eighty-two tips for stealing his heart? Is a group date being coordinated for all of them to go for sushi, or fondue? Will Cassie start crushing on Gates now? I move down the hall lost in these miserable thoughts, though I can't help looking up as I near Tyrick's locker. He's watching me with a funny, quizzical look on his face that makes me want to immediately turn around and walk the other way. Or better, evaporate.

"Is your friend okay?" he calls out.

I'm so surprised he's saying something nice, a lie springs out: "Oh, she has some extra credit to do for science."

"Got it," he says, like everything about all this is totally natural.

So that I don't ruin the moment by saying anything dumb (or give anyone else a chance to suspect Tyrick might be Pencil), I tell him I'll see him in class, and keep going.

He says, "Sounds good," and I just try not to have heart palpitations over the fact that this is the second time he's made a comment that proves he's been watching me in the mornings too. It pretty much means he must like me back, right?

Too bad the one person I could ask isn't around. And, worse, that I still miss her terribly, even though she's done something this awful.

I aim for the girls' room, where I can hide in a stall until the homeroom bell rings, so that nobody will hand me a pencil and ruin that one, tiny good moment with Tyrick I have to hold on to. As I'm about to duck in, though, someone grabs my shoulder. Someone with a grip so strong and bony it feels like she's wearing a chain-mail glove with metal tips on the fingers.

"I've got something for you," Izzy Gathing says behind me.

I turn around, hoping I don't appear the melted pudding-pop I've suddenly become inside. In her skinny, glittery, dark-purple-polished fingers, Izzy's clutching my diary. I want to snatch it from her and rub it down with Clorox wipes to get her nasty energy off it, even though I think that would ruin the marbled Italian paper of its cover.

"Of course," she adds, lifting one eyebrow in scorn, "from what we saw, you might want to just go on in there and flush it."

I reach out, not positive that she won't throw it over my head to a waiting member of her gang somewhere behind me, but she lets it go without hesitation. Relief surges through my whole body so fast I feel faint.

"Thank you," I say, unable to halt the manners Mom's drilled into Leelu and me. Not even to Izzy.

"Eh, don't worry." She shrugs, already half turned away. "We didn't read much, really. Too boring." Before she slinks into the flow of kids streaming past me at the sound of the homeroom bell, she gives me a wink and a little finger-diddle wave.

Watching after her, one hand still on the bathroom door, I know there are probably entire dictionaries dedicated to bad words for people like Izzy Gathing, but I'm too stunned and relieved to think of a single one.

Having my diary back is the biggest blessing in the world, but it's also a curse. I'm desperate to spend every second I get before and during classes flipping through the pages to guess what passages Kendra might've read, or see if they wrote anything awful in the margins. But I'm also terrified to take it out of my backpack, and have it snatched from me again. By lunch, however, all the hideous hypotheses in my head make it impossible not to look. So instead of sitting in my usual chair, I take a seat only a couple away from Yel and the basketball girls. They could all care less about Kendra, or me, or pretty much anything other than the women's NBA team, and they're all so gregarious I doubt anyone will notice I'm even there. I unpack my lunch and tuck my diary inside the covers of *Little Women*, hunching over nearly double, so that no one can see. It's nerve-rackingly risky, but I just can't bear the uncertainty anymore.

I flip fast through the earliest pages about the Divorce, hardly caring anymore if anyone saw that stuff. There is a play I forgot I wrote, recording the conversation Mom and I had about why she wasn't more upset with Dad when he left us, and, curious, I take a second to read it:

Mom: Just because I'm not hurting in front of you and your sister, that doesn't mean I don't feel it.

Me: But you never say anything bad about Daddy. Aren't you mad?

Mom: Sometimes, but what's happening between your father and me is between us. I don't need to drag you two into it. I need to take care of my own feelings, so that I can better help you take care of yours.

I pause. I still haven't told Mom about what's happened, partly because it's harder to tell her things in ten-minute phone updates when we're at Dad's, but also because I don't know *how* to explain—or even what to. Reading this almost feels like permission to keep the problem I'm having just between me and Cassie for a little while. At least until I'm sure.

One thing that *is* for sure, without a whole lot more reading, is that Cassie must've heard some of these bad things I wrote. Of course there are lots of good entries about her: earlier pages describing our various games, and a slew of poems about how silly she is. How much I love her, and love spending the night at her house instead of Dad's new house or Mom's condo. But those entries don't stand out nearly as much as the ones against Cassie do. I know her obsession with Kendra had been grating, but reading so *many* mean passages makes me feel terrible in a whole new way.

I really don't understand why Cassie admires Kendra so much, I wrote, not even two weeks ago. *She's not that special. We both know those kids have money and looks and nothing else. Sometimes, in Gates's case, not even looks. But maybe Cassie doesn't care any longer about being something more. Even with Lagoon she's more worried lately about does he think she's pretty, or that the "wrong" people will find out she likes him. Honestly, I worry she's getting a little bit shallow.*

And then another:

*Things I Would Rather Tell Cassie Than How Much I Like
Her New Red Plaid Flats (For the Sixtieth Time):*
   *You should be more confident about who you are, not
      what you wear.*
   *You sent me a photo the second you bought them—do you
      need me to show you my response again?*
   *Please stop watching so many runway shows, because
      you're forgetting that school is not supposed to be one
      of them.*

There's more, but I can't keep reading. I put my diary
safely back in my backpack and zip the pocket shut, not
wanting to look at it for a while. Kendra must have broadcast one of these entries on the bus, which means Cassie
heard these not-so-great thoughts of her own best friend
from someone who was *laughing* about them. While it
doesn't excuse the utter betrayal of ditching me for Kendra,
it does explain why she's not talking to me. She must have
felt terrible. Maybe she still does. Maybe she's waiting for
me to come to her. If I truly apologized, she might—

A sharp shriek of laughter rings over the general buzz
of the cafeteria, and around me people stretch up in their
chairs to see. There are more squeals, more giggles, and a

boy's voice saying "No way" floating from the hubbub. At Kendra's table.

If Cassie weren't sitting there, maybe I wouldn't care, but now I can't keep my eyes away. From four tables over it's a little hard to see without rising high out of my chair, until Billy Keegan stands up, dramatically lifting a milk-shake cup as though giving a toast, before chugging it down. I see Kendra and Neftali covering their faces in pretend horror. And then I hear Cassie's hysterical little giggle.

Yel looks over at me. "Gross."

"What are they doing?" I ask her.

She shrugs. "Smashing things together in Billy's milk shake and daring him to drink it, from the looks of it."

"That's stupid," I say. Although Cassie doesn't seem to think so.

The overhead lights glint in Yel's goggle-style glasses when she nods. "Sure is."

I feel the tiniest bit vindicated, but when I glance down at my still-untouched sandwich, I'm not certain I can eat anymore. It's not just because of what Billy might be digesting—it's the delighted way Cassie is laughing about it.

People are starting to get up and clear their trays anyway, so I start packing things up to eat later. Just as I'm putting my lunch sack into my backpack, I hear over me, "Hey, Fiona."

Azay Crowder is standing there, still holding his lunch tray. Two of his friends hover behind him. Azay is in my homeroom, and has never said a word to me before.

"Yes?"

"Saw you were doing a little reading." He nods toward my backpack, clearly knowing what's inside. "Wondered if I could borrow your book. I heard there was some pretty outrageous stuff in there."

Shame immediately burns my cheeks. I pull my backpack closer, afraid Azay might try and grab it, but he just laughs and walks away with his friends shuffling and guffawing behind him.

I know I wrote unkind things about Cassie, and I probably need to apologize, but none of that was as bad as her making me endure all of this.

Chapter Six

Everyone's hyper about the three-day weekend, but when Evie, Aja, and I load their overnight bags in the back of Maritza's Suburban, I don't think anyone feels quite as jubilant to have made it to Friday as I do.

"This is Maritza," I tell them, deciding at the last second not to refer to her as our sitter. "And that's my sister, Leelu."

"What a cute name!" Evie exclaims.

"It's after a Hawaiian princess," Leelu tells them proudly.

"Well, sort of," I correct. I love that Leelu thinks of herself as a princess, but it feels awkward in front of new friends, especially since it's not wholly true.

"Yeah-huh," she insists.

"Our parents thought the real name was a little too long," I explain, "so they created something of their own based on it."

"That's adorable," Evie coos.

"No wonder you're so creative," Aja says to me. "My mom got my name from some cheesy rock-star cartoon. Yours is from Shakespeare, right?"

I tell her it is, surprised to hear Aja being down on a name that to me seems mysterious and exotic. Still, it's nice she thinks I'm creative.

"We are waiting for Cassie?" Maritza asks.

Aja makes a choking sound in her throat.

"Um, Cassie has other plans this weekend," I say. Aja nudges me with her elbow and we trade sneaky looks. It doesn't exactly feel good, but it's better than most of what I've felt this week.

"Do you want to do a quiz?" Leelu holds up her *Sleepover Secrets Handbook*, which she must have had at school all day, just for this. Most people would be annoyed to have their little sister horning in on their sleepover, but Leelu's games and ideas are another thing that got us both through the Divorce. Having a best friend who got my attachment to my sister without me having to explain it was part of what made Cassie so great, too. She automatically understood that when there's a nine-year-old around, you don't have to feel too old to be silly and free. So I'm relieved when right away Evie says she'd love to. Aja looks a little skeptical, but she's at least willing.

And of course within three minutes, Leelu wins them both over.

"Your sister is priceless," Aja tells me when we get to Room for Dessert to pick out treats for later. "You're so lucky to have such a cutie around who idolizes you. My sisters all can't wait until I'm grown-up and going to college or being boring having babies like them."

"I know," Evie adds. "I have a little sister too—well, stepsister—and she's nothing but annoying. Aja's lucky at least two of hers don't live in the same house."

Leelu is so much more than adorable or annoying to me, but I'm curious about what it would be like having an older sister. I want to know more about Evie's home life, too. Asking the two of them questions about their families also helps distract me from the sudden surprising alarm I feel, being at Cassie's and my favorite dessert place for the first time without her.

When Aja and Evie start debating between lemon or turtle bars (I'm on Evie's side about turtle, but don't want to get between them), I move over to Leelu. Together we peer into the case at our old favorites and the new additions this month.

"Cookie-dough brownie," Leelu points, looking at me expectantly.

"Maybe we should try something different this time." The cookie-dough brownie is what Cassie and I always share. "What do you think?"

Leelu stares hard into the case. Finally she points, smiling. Fruity Rice Krispies treats won't have quite the same decadence, but at least they're bright and colorful like my sister.

When we make it home through the holiday weekend traffic, Leelu and I give my friends a tour of the house. Evie oohs in almost every room, which is funny, because while Dad's new house is nice, it's not as nice as Cassie's, and definitely not as nice as our old house. Even I can admit that the big entertainment room is a bonus, though, and when Aja asks if we can search for some music video she wants to show us, I tell her to be my guest.

"'Try the gray stuff; it's delicious!'" she sings, doing a jaunty little dance step.

"I love that movie!" Leelu cheers. "Except *Frozen* is better."

I'm still shocked Aja knows *Beauty and the Beast* at all, or would admit she did in such a cheesy way. "I didn't think anyone else liked vintage Disney except—" I stop myself from saying "Cassie" in time. "Except me and, um, Leelu."

Evie and Aja look at each other, trading excited grins. "Are you kidding?" Aja says. "Evie, show them that *Fantasia* mash-up we found."

As we huddle around the screen of Aja's phone, the back of my head relaxes. Cassie always insisted we keep our Disney obsession between us and Leelu. Suddenly not being self-conscious about it, and realizing I might be able to find other friends who like the same things my sister and I do, feels really good. I help Evie call up the internet on our giant screen with the remote, and we spend the rest of the time before Dad gets home going from watching cool Disney-inspired clips to eventually bobbing around to a bunch of performances by this neat musician Aja really likes—a girl with a super-sultry voice but who always wears a suit and tie.

It's already been a great afternoon, and Dad's treat to drive us to Carmel-by-the-Sea for dinner only makes it better. There, we'll get to enjoy our gourmet pizza place, Allegro, but the cute little cottages (Leelu calls them fairy hobbit apartments) and stunning blue water are also always so relaxing.

"I don't think we're at Domino's anymore, Eve," Aja

says sideways to Evie when she looks at Allegro's menu.

"I know," I hear Evie whisper back. "Fiona's so lucky to be rich."

I pretend I don't hear, because first of all my dad isn't *that* rich, and secondly Evie's awe makes me suddenly feel different from her and Aja in a way I wasn't before. Cassie was mean to make fun of Evie in the library, but spending more close-up time with her helps me see how "oh gosh" about everything she can be. For example, she's so over-whelmed by all the choices, it takes her forever to choose anything on the menu. In the end she just splits the arti-choke pizza Aja orders.

Still, for a first outing with new friends, it's a good evening. Until, in the car on the way home, Leelu starts explaining the rules for True Voice Dancing. I love this game, but even after the Disney bonding earlier, there could be a limit to how much little-girlishness someone like Aja can take. The second we're back at the house, though, she's asking Leelu to show her what the dress-up clothes are all about. So we get the karaoke machine set up, and Leelu's practically bouncing off the walls over the fact that we'll have two actual judges this time instead of a row of Barbies. It takes a few minutes of trying to get her to calm down and act normal before I realize Evie's got this weird look on her face.

"Do we really have to sing—alone?" She's biting the edge of her lip.

"Oh no. Just lip-synch."

That doesn't help her. "Can I just be the judge?"

Leelu whips around from where she's peering into the dress-up trunk. "Everybody has to go. It's the rule."

"But what if—"

"I'll pick a good one for you," Aja reassures Evie. "One you know. It'll be fun. Or we can do a duet."

That helps Evie relax a little, but she still refuses to perform until the rest of us have, which seems weird, since she doesn't mind singing in chorus. Once she sees that no one could look more spastic than my little sister when she's fake belting Tina Turner while gliding around in an old party dress of Mom's, though, Evie cheers and claps and eventually she's laughing so hard at Aja's performance that I think she's going to hyperventilate.

To my surprise, TVD with Aja and Evie is even more fun than with Cassie. Cassie's always stopping us in the middle of a song, correcting our performances and saying to start over, treating it like a real TV show instead of a game. But Aja and Evie let loose just like my sister. At the end, when Leelu is (of course) proclaimed the winner, Aja takes a selfie of the four of us and posts it right away without having to retake it five more times like Cassie would.

It's so liberating I don't even care if Cassie sees it somehow.

It's late by then, so we change into our pajamas and settle down for a movie.

"What about *Into the Woods*?" I suggest. If Aja likes Disney, she might appreciate this too.

"Oooh." Aja claps her hands. "It's not that scary," she reassures Evie.

I go to the kitchen for the desserts we picked out earlier, and then we pile up the couch pillows and splay out. Leelu falls asleep within the first ten minutes like usual, but that's a good thing because the movie is pretty dark after all. At this one part when Meryl Streep is being particularly ugly, Aja goes, "Well, hi there, Cassie Parker," and stretches across the cushions to high-five me. Evie giggles, but checks my expression to see what I think. Aja doesn't know what a good listener Cassie is, or everything we've been through together, but sitting here in my big entertainment room, with my cute little sister curled up next to me, and a new friend who's so sophisticated she doesn't care what anyone thinks about her, I don't feel bad at all.

"So did you have a good time?" Mom wants to know when she checks in on Saturday night.

"It was fun," I tell her.

"And does Cassie like them as much too?"

"She doesn't know them as well."

I don't know why I'm still not telling Mom that Cassie wasn't there. Or that she dumped me in front of the whole cafeteria to sit with the awful girls who stole my diary. Maybe it's because I'd rather cling for a little while to the good feeling of having Evie and Aja over. How nice it was not to feel shy about being silly in front of people other than Cassie, or how great it was to do the fun things she and I used to, without also having to talk about Kendra, or look at fashion boards on Pinterest that I'm not that interested in. Besides, I still don't know how to make sense of what happened between us to a grown-up who will want to come in and fix everything. I don't know how to explain the alien feeling of having a good time without my best friend. Besides, maybe Cassie will still call me tomorrow.

Luckily, even on a Saturday night Mom likes to keep our check-ins short, so she doesn't push.

Still, my inability to talk to Mom about what's happening brings Cassie right back to the forefront of my mind, and it's much harder to dismiss her the way Aja thinks I should. All weekend I hear nothing from her—making this the longest we've ever gone without talking or texting. I can't help but wonder if Cassie's too embarrassed to reach out to me. It'd be terrible if our friendship was ruined forever because of pride. Especially with only two weeks of school left, before we plunge into summer and could be needlessly separated for months. Maybe if I'm the one to make the first move, we can get things resolved and there won't be anything I have to explain to Mom at all.

Even if I'm willing to try something like that, it's still important to know for sure if that's what Cassie wants before I make a fool out of myself, so back at school Tuesday morning I decide to utilize our *Harriet the Spy* tactics for some Cassie stalking. It's much less fun on my own, and I have to keep a pretty big distance—I *really* can't have Izzy catching me lurking around, let alone Cassie. Being way too paranoid to write anything out in my diary anymore complicates things even further. I take notes on a small spiral notepad instead, and tape them in the pages of my diary when I get home. It just isn't safe to bring it to school, and I feel weird about writing too much in it for some reason. Over the course of the week, though, I assemble a few crucial tidbits:

She went shopping over the holiday weekend. New white leather jacket looks expensive. (Note: What rewards from her GPA/chore competition with Tom did she forfeit to get something so extravagant? Memorial Day sale K took her to?) Also new ankle boots like the rest of them: cowboy-saddle brown, though, and not as fancy. Boots worn 3x this week. Note from outfit 6/1 (black-and-white striped tunic, rose-print scarf, leggings, flats): likely she intended to wear leather jacket 2nd time, but decided at the last minute not to.

Completely abandoned any hallway activity involving Lagoon. First couple days assumed she'd given up her crush, until 5/31 seen staring after him in the cafeteria while he was clearing trash, everyone at K's table busy soothing Neftali (over something ridiculous).

Sits in the courtyard with K's gang every day before school, but K makes C walk two steps behind while they travel there from the bus. Also (throwback to third grade for some reason? Initiation rites?), C sits on the cement wall beside K's table instead of on bench, even when there's room. (Note: need better vantage point than the far windows across courtyard in hidden spot from 6th grade wing if to investigate/understand further.)

C does not seem to mind either of above. Watches new friends' faces and reacts with perfect laughter/distress/ other called-for emotion. Telltale signs C loves this new situation: Sits up very straight w/ knees together. Casts brief, but happy glances beneath her lashes around the courtyard, making sure people notice who she's sitting with. She is definitely now in their group.

Most hopeful AND despairing observation: C clearly

upset seeing me in science. Arrives daily just seconds before
the late bell, looking purposefully away from my seat. Two
bright red spots on her cheekbones, and (if hair in ponytail
or bun, or neck otherwise exposed) back of her neck also
red. Meaning: angry, mixed with embarrassed. Never
turns in my direction, even if instructed to change seats for
group work or look at classification posters at the back of
the room by teacher.

Conclusions:

C avoiding me. But by revealing discomfort,
acknowledges I exist. What's happening between us makes
her unhappy. At least agitated. Still no action taken to
cross divide in spite of easy proximity, however.

None of these observations make it any easier to talk about
it all week, so I avoid the subject of Cassie altogether while
we're back over at Mom's place. The information I've gathered is a little too confusing, anyway. There are times,
during my spying, when I'll catch Cassie looking off into
space, or obviously faking a laugh, when it seems she isn't
that happy with her new situation and might text me the
second school is over. Other days, her radiant delight in all
things Kendra twists my insides with jealousy and despair.
I try to stay away from online stuff for that same reason,
but it's impossible because I'm constantly wondering what

secrets they're sharing, if they've invented their own language, what new games they have. All they post are selfies or pictures of each other, though. Still, I stare at them, wondering what Cassie's said about me, or if she's said anything at all.

By chorus on Friday afternoon, I'm itchy and edgy—not even seeing Tyrick first thing in the morning has the same thrill it did when I was with Cassie. I'm not sure how to improve my mental state at all, especially since I still can't bring myself to write in my diary, and worse, Mom has a floor show of a bunch of importers to attend, where she'll be looking for new furnishings for her clients. Leelu and I have to tag along with her, so there'll be no chance to distract myself with anything fun like last weekend.

Next to me, Evie slaps her music folder against her chair and huffs, "Uch."

Instantly I'm glad not to be alone in this bad feeling. "You too?"

She flops down, shoulders drooping over and legs splayed out. "Spirit Week," she groans.

In spite of the intercom announcements, posters, and school-wide email blasts, I've been so focused on Cassie that I forgot all about it.

"The last thing I want to think about during the final week of school is how much I love school," Evie says. "I want to think about how much I want to get *out* of school. And never come back."

"You don't have to participate, you know."

"Except if you don't, you look like a nobody."

Evie means that if you don't, all the popular people—who *love* Spirit Week, and go all out for each day's theme—will make you feel stupid for not doing the same.

An idea hits me. "What if you did the opposite?"

Her brow crinkles.

"I mean, what if we did," I correct. "What if every day of Spirit Week next week, instead of something like Rock Star Day, we wear the exact opposite."

"You mean have on San Carlos colors the last day instead?"

I grin. "You got it."

"Gosh, Fee. That's—"

My smile curls into something that feels almost as cunning as one of Cassie's after we've concocted another great collaboration. She may be living her dream of being part of the trendy crowd now, but from what I've observed, that mainly looks demeaning and stressful. Thanks to Aja and Evie, I'm not afraid of sticking out anymore. At least, not as much. And, besides, I've found a project to help me get through another weekend without Cassie around.

"It's brilliant, right?"

Chapter Seven

vie and Aja go crazy over my Reverse Spirit Week idea. With five different outfits to coordinate, suddenly there are a ton of opinions between the three of us, none of them melding as smoothly as when Cassie and I invented something together. Immediately after school on Friday, Evie sends me and Aja a bajillion updates from a Pinterest board she's making of punk rock outfits, until Aja reminds her that on Dress Like a Rock Star Day, we're actually going as grandmas. There's so much back-and-forth in not even an hour, I feel almost as confused and distracted as Mom gets when her clients are in a decorating frenzy.

By the time dinner's over, it's clear that it'll be way easier if we can plan together in the same place, so before

Mom settles in to read Leelu and me our bedtime chapter, I ask if our neighbor's son Julio can come "watch" us while Mom's in Santa Cruz at her show. Julio graduated from college last spring, but he still lives with his mom, Mrs. Carroll, and sometimes babysits after Maritza's hours, or helps with the tiny excuse we have for a yard.

"I love Julio!" Leelu exclaims, arranging her stuffed animals around her.

I forgot to factor in my sister. "You still have to go with Mom."

Immediately she begins to yowl. "How come Fiona gets to stay home? I hate those things." She squeezes her hands into fists. "They're so boring!"

I don't want Leelu to have to go either, but my friends and I need to focus, and I'm just not sure she won't be a distraction, especially if this is her immediate reaction.

"Leeluni September, you know that isn't how we communicate what we want in this house," Mom says, before addressing me. "Wouldn't this all be easier to do at Cassie's? I'll text Serena. I'm sure Tom will be at home. We can even pay him some extra babysitting money."

The combination of my sister's painful wailing, my mom's sudden exasperation, plus her assumption that Cassie would be involved throws me off guard.

"Um. We can't."

"But why ever not?" She tells Leelu to be quiet or else she'll really be punished.

"Because we're doing it on different teams," I blurt. "And it, ah, has to be a surprise. Leelu can help," I throw in, if only to make Mom stop asking about Cassie. I can tell her the whole story later, when she's a little less stressed and we're not in the middle of an unexpected Leelu meltdown.

Immediately Leelu looks hopeful at me. "I can take notes."

"Or something," I say. "Mom, please? We need to do this fast."

"You're the one to call Julio." Mom points a finger at me. "And you"—she aims a disapproving eye at Leelu—"are absolutely under your sister's watch, and if I hear even the tiniest complaint from her, it's no screens for a week."

Leelu puts on a sheepish face and nods. I know my own is mimicking hers.

"All right," Mom says, taking a breath and opening the book to our marker. "Now let's try to get settled, girls, shall we?"

Miraculously, everything comes together. I make all the necessary calls on Saturday morning, and luckily, everyone can come over that afternoon, including Julio. He hangs out in our living room on his phone, while the four of us pile on Leelu's and my twin beds and make our plans. It was silly of me to worry about Leelu being a distraction. She takes careful notes on her unicorn-covered clipboard, to keep us organized while we brainstorm and talk, and even offers up some fantastic treasures from her dress-up trunk. Her suggestions for International Day and Future You Day are priceless, too. Once again I'm grateful my sister makes such a great partner, even if she is two and a half years younger.

By the time Aja's dad comes to pick my friends up at three, we've made copies on Mom's printer of our final outfit lineup, complete with any action points we still need to accomplish. I'm still not putting down any real feelings in my diary, but it's weird not to record anything about such a big, productive day, so I tape in our list:

Day One: Dress to the Nines Day
[SCHOOL: Pajama Day]
    —as over-the-top fancy as you can get!!
    —don't forget makeup if you have any

Day Two: International Day
[SCHOOL: All-American Day]
    —make T-shirts with Sharpies or fabric paint for favorite flag of a foreign country:

Aja: Democratic Republic of the Congo
Evie: Brazil
Fiona: Haiti or France (?)
—Speak in foreign accents all day?
—Bring lunch that matches country?

Day Three: Dress Like a Grandma Day
[SCHOOL: Dress Like a Rock Star Day]
—find old nightgowns, robes, slippers, old dresses?
Curlers?
—Aja: get that walker out of the garage from Grandpa
Ned's stay

Day Four: Future You Day
[SCHOOL: Retro Day]
—Aja: music-executive/mega-pop-star combo
—Evie: still not decided. Astronaut?
—Fiona: famous author; re-cover favorite books with
titles that have her name on them

Day Five: Rival Spirit Day
[SCHOOL: School Spirit Day]
—yellow and white outfits!! Go San Carlos!!
— don't forget your yearbooks if you haven't brought
them all week

Final note: partnering with Leeluni September + new
(fantastic) friends = I don't miss Cassie one single bit.

All the other students get so excited about the idea of wearing pajamas to school, but I think it's much more fun that Evie, Aja, and I are going over-the-top fancy. Aja has a long formal dress she wore to her cousin's black-tie wedding, and though Evie feels shy that she only has an eyelet sundress, I know that draped in the dozens of long fake pearl strands Leelu gave her, she'll look great. I decided on the green taffeta dress I wore for the Women in Business gala where Mom got that award, since Tyrick's favorite color is green. Though I've apparently escaped the danger of him finding out my secret, I still want him to notice me.

Securing Leelu's old tiara on top of my head, I can't wait to parade around for the first time as part of an original-looking group, instead of being a ho-hum joiner in flannel pants with the cuffs dragging under some raggedy slippers. Cassie and I would never have had the nerve to do something like this just the two of us, but like Aja said over the weekend, this will definitely make an impression, and with her around I know that's a good thing. Maybe we'll even convince some other kids to do the opposite during the week, like Aja hopes River and his friends might. Which would mean maybe even Tyrick too, since he hangs out with them.

Mom whistles when I step into the hall in my fancy finery, and Leelu claps her approval, but on the way to school I'm still grateful to be getting dropped off instead of having to ride the bus. I want to stand out—but maybe not very first thing in the morning.

"Cassie certainly will be surprised," Mom says as she pulls up to the curb. "I haven't seen you this dressed up in a while."

"We wanted to have an impact." I try to sound nonchalant like Aja, instead of nervous. The way Mom's saying it, maybe I'm too dressed up.

"Promise to take pictures," Leelu demands.

"Oh, we will."

There's an anxious prickle all over me as I open the door. It's too late to back out now, even if the idea is starting to feel a little silly, but at least, I remind myself, I won't be silly on my own. I give Mom and Leelu my best Duchess Kate wave as they drive off, and once they're out of sight, I turn to my destination. For the first time since Cassie joined forces with Kendra, at least I know for sure where I'm going. Instead of spying on the courtyards, or doing anything Cassie-related, I go straight for the chorus room, where Aja, Evie, and I agreed to meet, so that we can parade to our homerooms together. There are a few strange looks thrown my way as I walk, but with each step in my sparkly sandals I feel increasingly outstanding—all pizazzed up in things I hardly ever get to wear, while the rest of the school looks so slouchy.

My mood lifts even higher when I make it to the chorus room. Evie and Aja are already there, and I was right that the strands and strands of pearls on Evie are fantastic.

"I was just about to give Evie some sparkle," Aja says, spilling feathers from the red boa around her neck as she pulls me over to a chair in the front row. While she spreads glittery stuff on Evie's eyelids and lips, we talk over each other, relaying our mornings and what it was like walking into school. Several other girls come over as we sit there— some I've never talked to before—saying Dress to the Nines Day is way better than pajamas.

When Aja finishes with her own makeup, she looks like she's about to walk the red carpet instead of the seventh grade hallway, and if I look half as fabulous as she does, I really can't wait to get to our lockers.

First, though, we need pictures. Handing our phones to other chorus girlfriends, we make silly dramatic poses for our personal collection, but also some cute ones for posting later. Then it's time to head out, with sopranos and altos giggling in our sashaying wake.

"Oh my gosh, people are looking," Evie squeaks the minute we round the corner and the main corridor comes into view.

"Of course they're looking." Aja holds her head higher and smiles at a group of sixth graders slinking past us with band cases. "We look spectacular."

I make a mental note to write that word down somewhere later, because it's absolutely the right one to describe my feeling as the three of us enter the crowd. Even a couple of eighth graders smile or jerk their chins up in appreciation of our outfits, and as we push open the doors to the seventh grade wing, it feels like making an entrance to some kind of glamorous party that only we got invited to.

"Let's go say hi to the boys," Aja says, emboldened by her silky dress and dramatic eye makeup. She strides down the hall straight for River's locker, where he and a couple of friends are hanging around, including—yikes—Tyrick. I'm not sure about being this bold (and Evie clearly wants to turn right around too), but Aja's so commanding we have no choice but to follow.

"Hi," she says, smiling straight at River.

His friend with braces makes an *ooh* face.

"What are you supposed to be?" Tyrick asks her, like he doesn't even see me standing there.

"What're *you*?" Aja says back, eyeing him with disapproval.

"I can't tell if those are pajamas, or it's just dirty laundry week at your house."

The boys make noises of *she got you*, grinning and shoving at each other, but Tyrick smiles sheepishly, almost as if he's pleased by her insult.

"So are you saying you sleep in that?" River asks.

Aja smiles big, ready with her comeback. She snaps her fingers and raises them up over her head in a perfect mambo pose. "Not me. I'm up dancing all night long," she says, before pulling me and Evie away with her in a flurry of satin.

We keep our giggles in until we reach the safety of my locker at the other end of the hall, where we collapse into various stages of hilarity and embarrassment. Even Aja has her hands over her mouth, bent double with laughing.

"Did you see his face?" she says, shoulders shaking.

"Aja, I can't believe you." Evie's high-pitched voice makes it hard to tell whether she's angry or not.

"I can't believe it, either," Aja admits. "It just came out. I don't know—maybe it's this dress or something." She strikes another pose, though not one so dramatic. "It makes me feel sassy and outrageous."

"You don't need a dress like that to be outrageous," Evie tells her.

"Yeah, I don't know if I can take Supermodel Aja on top

of regular Aja," I tease, hoping that joking will cover up the unexpected uneasiness I feel about what just happened. Though Aja's rather hard not to notice in general, Tyrick was so focused on her he barely even acknowledged my existence.

"This is so fun!" Evie squeals, her dimply grin sparkling even more than her glittery makeup.

"I know," Aja agrees. "And it's all thanks to Fiona. I would never have—"

She's cut off by a loud, mock-shocked voice coming toward us down the hall: "What is this? Some kind of Dork Disney Princess convention?"

It freezes all of us.

"Don't look," Aja whispers, eyes on the approaching gang.

But I don't have to, even though I can't help glancing as they pass. I'd still know Cassie's voice anywhere, and I definitely recognize Kendra's and Izzy's cackles of approval. As they glide by together in a collection of Lululemon yoga pants and designer nightgowns, someone—I think it's Cheyenne—mutters an insult about dress-up being for kindergarten, and one of the boys says something about this not being prom. I'm trying to ignore them. Or at least look like I am. But still I can't help seeing Gates, bending in a deep and phony bow to us, wearing teddy-bear-print footie pajamas that I can't believe they make in a size big enough to fit.

There are no words in me for a clever comeback. It'd be nice to say they look ridiculous, but really they're the coolest Pajama Day ever, and I feel like a fool. Aja's trying to act like it doesn't matter, but even she's eyeing her boa with doubt.

The stronger version of me would ask who cares what Kendra's gang thinks, and maybe somewhere inside I don't, but it wasn't her who said that awful thing. It was Cassie.

When the homeroom bell rings over our heads, the three of us split up, not saying anything—not even *see you later*. I'm so mad and disappointed, in homeroom I take out my English notebook without caring about pencils or mean comments. I may be too afraid to bring my diary to school, and there's a chance someone will still tease me or steal this, but if how I'm feeling right now somehow got back to Cassie, I wouldn't care anymore, anyway.

To: Cassie Parker
From: Fiona Coppleton
Date: June 2016
Re: Being Called a Dork Disney Princess by the Number One President of That Fan Club, even if No One Else Knows It

Dear Cassie:

You may not care anymore, but I am writing to formally exterminate our friendship for now and evermore. I thought maybe you missed me, and maybe I missed you, but after what you pulled in the hallway, I can't ever be your friend again. I hope you are happy with your new ones, though I'm convinced you've become even worse than them.

I don't care if they're mean to you. I hope they're mean to you, because if I hated anything, I think I hate you right now. And not even for the reasons you think. I don't hate you for not defending me against K on the bus, or not getting my diary back. I don't even hate you for ditching me for your new group. Well, maybe a little. But you can have K and her gang—you deserve each other. What I hate you most for—what I will never ever forget that you did—is ruining something that was fun for me and my new friends, all to make yourself look better than us.

So that's it, Cassie Parker. We are finished forever.

With gravest sincerity,

Your former friend,

Fiona

Chapter Eight

After that, everything goes wrong.

And it's all Cassie's fault.

By chorus, even though I've gotten some compliments on my dress and my jewels, it seems like people are saying it in more of a teasing way than not, and as soon as I walk into the room I notice Aja's not wearing her boa anymore. Evie's down to only one short strand of pearls, too.

"That thing was itching my neck is all." Aja tilts her chin and shakes her glittery earrings as we get our music folders. "It's still fun."

I nod in agreement, though I can't wait to put on jeans myself, and forget the whole day.

There's no further mention of tomorrow—what's

supposed to be International Day for us, while everyone else dresses in patriotic gear. When Leelu asks about it the next morning, I toss my homemade French flag T-shirt onto her bed, telling her since it was her idea, she should wear it. I pull on cord capris and a T-shirt with glow-in-the-dark fireworks on it, which feels slightly American, in case anyone cares. International is still way cooler, but I know, after yesterday, none of us wants to stand out anymore.

"What happened to *Les Misérables?*" Mom wants to know when I enter the kitchen.

"We didn't think anyone would get it."

She makes a sound like "Is that so?" and hands me a plate of buttered cinnamon raisin toast before sitting down to check her email while I eat.

"Everything seemed so urgent over the weekend," she says after a few moments.

"Yes, well, after—"

"Hang on, Fiona. Leelu, you really need to get down here!" she hollers. Mom had dinner with some Chicago clients who were in town last night, which meant Maritza stayed late, and we didn't get to talk about what happened with Cassie. In the light of a new morning, though, yesterday feels too mortifying to say out loud.

Mom turns her attention back to me. "Well, last week of school. I hope it's still fun. Your dad said he made reservations at Sardine Factory for Friday?"

I nod. Dad gets us for the last day of school this year, because Mom had us last time.

"And we'll celebrate together later, too."

Another nod from me. The Sardine Factory is my favorite, but I'm not feeling very celebratory these days.

"Do you want to do something special here with Cassie, or is she part of dinner on Friday?" She cocks her ear toward the hall, trying to listen for sounds of my sister stirring. "Leelu, this is not a drill."

"I think Cassie has different plans."

Mom looks surprised. "Is everything okay?"

I don't know what to say. Because suddenly it absolutely isn't—not what happened with my diary, or Cassie abandoning me, or the nasty way she treated my friends and me—but I also have a sense, the way I'm suddenly getting beamed with alert-Mom attention, that if I admit what happened, the first thing Mom'll do is call Cassie's mom, try to arrange some kind of intervention or truce between us. And if Cassie's making fun of me for dressing up like a princess, the humiliation of our moms getting involved would be far worse than having my diary read out loud. Maybe. Besides, we have to leave in about seven minutes, and if Leelu doesn't get downstairs right now, she and Mom will be at it again.

"I'll go get Leelu," I offer instead, sliding out of my chair.

I try not to let Cassie dominate my final week of school, but it turns out to be impossible. For one thing, when I go to post the cute pic of me, Aja, and Evie in our fancy finery (because it *was* fun, and I'm not going to let anyone rob me of that), right off I see a new photo of Cassie cheek to cheek with Izzy, the caption saying *You don't have to wear a tiara to be queen!* There are more of her with Kendra, and the other girls, but the worst are a bunch of pictures from her grandmother's wedding this weekend, including several group shots in which there's a girl who must be her new cousin, Lana. Cassie had been so worried about Tess getting married, especially to someone like Howie, whom Cassie barely knew, but she was optimistic about finally having a cousin her age. Now it's already happened, but I didn't get to hear about any of it. From the pictures of everyone dancing and smiling, though, it's obvious Cassie's more than fine, and why wouldn't she be? Not only is she now part of the most envied group in school, but she has a new family member to replace me with, too. They're even wearing the same fantastic dress.

I have to watch her the rest of the week in real life, parading around with her new friends in their matching

Spirit Week uniforms, acting up in the halls and the cafeteria with even more obnoxiousness than usual.

On the last day of school, instead of separate lunch periods, all the classes have a giant picnic out on the soccer field. Aja, Evie, and I sit together, dutifully wearing school colors without having talked about it, like none of us ever heard of Reverse Spirit Week, and I try not to look at Kendra passing out big helium balloons to all her friends (including Cassie, of course) from a giant bouquet she had delivered to campus. Evie spends a long time filling an entire page in my yearbook with her giant bubbly script, and while she does Aja and I make plans to go to the mall next week before she visits her uncle in Seattle, but I can't help feeling bitter. This isn't how things were supposed to go. This isn't how I'm supposed to feel. Even when Tyrick signed my yearbook in English, all I could think was that there isn't anyone to show it to who knows or cares. He only wrote *Nice knowing ya—have a good summer*, anyway, which he probably writes in everyone's.

Behind us a squeal interrupts my thoughts, and when I look over, a bunch of eighth graders have their arms around each other, hugging. Some of them are even crying: sad and excited to be moving on to high school. At first I think they look ridiculous, until I realize next year, I'll be one of them.

And I'll be darned if I'm going to feel anywhere near as bad as this then.

Luckily, I still have Leelu.

"We're going to the boardwalk!" she shouts the minute I get to Maritza's car at the end of the day. And while I can't quite get to her level of bounciness about it yet, the combination of sunshine, cotton candy, and booths of souvenirs all remind me of summers before I even knew Cassie—back way before the Divorce—when Leelu and I were little. When we wore fairy wings every day, including to weekly story time at the library, or for the daytime movies with our old nanny, Romella. We swam in the neighborhood pool every afternoon, Dad grilled out almost every night whether Mom had to work or not, and we still had a real family. Watching the beach breeze stir the tips of the zillion tiny braids Leelu has scooped in a pony on top of her head, I'm so grateful to have her to always help me through rough times.

"Let's get our faces painted," I suggest, as we pass by a booth decorated with streamers and pictures of different possibilities. I want to do something symbolic. Something Cassie wouldn't be caught dead doing anymore, but that Leelu will still love. Without much begging on our part, Maritza says yes and we're all three picking out patterns:

orange, gold, and black tiger designs for Maritza; snowflake swirls and sparkles for Leelu; and a trellis of glittery roses to climb up my cheek. We post pictures and Leelu and I skip together in the sunshine, licking ice cream cones.

Just as I thought it would, my bitterness is already starting to melt.

Dad's home when we get back, and though he loves our decorated faces, he tells us with a mischievously arched eyebrow to wash everything off and hurry into dinner clothes, even though it's only five thirty.

"A surprise!" Leelu claps, bouncing down the hall to our bathroom. Dad wanting to take us out on the last day of school isn't that much of a surprise, but we excitedly help each other into our dresses anyway, speculating what beyond the Sardine Factory he might have in store.

"Maybe he's taking us to San Francisco," Leelu says hopefully. Leelu's class did a project on Alcatraz last month, and she's been curious about it ever since.

"Not tonight, silly. It's too long a trip. But we could go this summer."

"And roller-skating?"

"Absolutely."

I move to my desk, going automatically for my diary, but at the last second take out the more anonymous notepad

I've been using instead. School's over, and there's no chance of anyone teasing me about my diary for another three months, but the idea of writing in it still feels dangerous. "Let's make a list."

We go into the living room, where we can sit without rumpling our dresses.

"We should have some sort of project or challenge," Leelu says, leaning back against the fluffy white cushions of Dad's giant couch. "Like, you know, summer reading or something. Where we get rewards."

I write it down, thinking that's something Cassie would come up with. Or, at least, used to.

"You put down roller-skating, right?"

I nod, adding it.

"And!" Her face goes from serious to playful. "How about we do one of those—"

The doorbell startles us both.

"Would one of you please get that?" Dad calls from his bedroom in the back. "I'm just finishing up."

And right away I know who it is.

"Well hellooo there, beauties," Jennifer coos when Leelu flings open the door. I thought Leelu was silly for thinking Dad might take us to San Francisco tonight, but I feel silly for not imagining that his "happy" surprise would be something involving Jennifer. In the doorway, she stoops and kisses Leelu on the forehead instead of giving her a hug, because her arms are full of presents.

I let go of my notebook and let it slip forgotten to the floor.

"What's all that?" Leelu asks, jouncing on her toes.

"Just a few things to congratulate you two on all your school successes. We'll wait for your father. Is he ready yet?"

"Hello there," Dad says, hurrying to give Jennifer a kiss on the cheek. "What do we have here?" He indicates the packages like he's surprised, but I can tell by the way they're looking at each other that this is the entire reason we had to be ready by five thirty.

"Just a couple of things for the girls."

Jennifer moves around to the couch to sit down, pressing her knees together. She's a lawyer, like Dad, though she practices contract law, not the expensive divorce cases my dad handles all the time. Still, to me she dresses more like she hopes someone will cast her on some reality show. She keeps wanting to take Leelu and me to get the same kind of expensive weave she likes, but Dad says Leelu's too young, and I just say I won't until Leelu can. Jennifer indulges in big jewelry, too (chunky necklaces, gemstone earrings round as quarters), so it's no surprise that the first thing she has Leelu and me open are semi-matching sparkling bracelets. Leelu's beads and charms are in mostly icicle blue, mine in green.

"There's room to add more charms, of course." Jennifer smiles wide. "For all your special new memories. Hopefully some we make together."

I don't watch her and Dad trade happy glances, or admit that it's nice of her to have noticed I've been wearing more green lately. Cassie would be jealous of something like this too, which makes me feel proud and lonely at the same time.

I pretend to be so interested in examining each charm that I forget to say anything.

Or notice how Leelu gives Jennifer an extra-long thank-you hug, asks for her help putting the bracelet on, and then rubs noses with her in the way I thought only we did.

"Well, we'd better get a move on," Dad says, smoothing his pants.

"But I want the rest." Leelu stamps her foot.

"You're really too old for that kind of act."

"After dinner, princess," Jennifer adds over Dad's gentle scolding. Like she suddenly knows how to soothe Leelu's temper better than the two of us.

But Leelu looks at Jennifer like she's Tiana come to life, and prances beside her to the car ahead of me and Dad. On the way it's clear she's forgotten all about our list of summer to-dos, and instead listens intently to Dad's answers when

Jennifer asks him about his own last-day-of-school memories. Which makes him ask her to tell us some of hers, too. I like hearing Dad's stories myself, but the three of them are so far down nostalgia lane, Dad hardly even asks us about our own days.

At least at the restaurant he's made sure to get a table by the window, and right away orders crab cakes plus two plates of their famous cheese bread—Leelu's and my favorites. Jennifer doesn't like sourdough, so she doesn't have any, but I don't feel sorry.

Still, I'm trying not to sulk. I'm trying to enjoy my favorite restaurant with Dad and Leelu even if Jennifer has to be here.

But then Dad reaches for her hand. "We have some good news," he says.

"I did some juggling around," Jennifer picks up, "and thanks to my boss and a couple of meetings that can become conference calls . . ." She looks at Dad.

"Jennifer will be joining us in Disneyland," he says for her.

Leelu jumps out of her seat and claps. "Really!?"

"But that's our trip with Cassie," I blurt, not caring at the moment that of course Cassie isn't coming.

Dad frowns a little. "My understanding is that Cassie can't join us, Fiona."

Dad and I haven't talked about Cassie at all, so I'm not sure how he knows this.

He sees my confusion. "I had to email Serena to finalize some things about the hotel, and when I did she told me that unfortunately Cassie had something come up for that week. Since you and Cassie are so close, I believed you knew."

"Well, what came up?" I try to sound prideful instead of embarrassed. It hadn't occurred to me Dad would talk to Serena about Cassie and Disneyland, but of course he'd have to.

"She didn't say." Dad looks sorry. "It's my mistake for not mentioning it, but I really didn't think it was necessary. You can see, I hope, that it's all working out just fine. Now instead of having to make cancellations, Jennifer is taking Cassie's place. Yes?"

"Does that mean we'll have the same room?" Leelu asks. "Do we get to share a bed?" Her eager smile is aimed at Jennifer, not me.

Jennifer looks like Leelu just turned a pumpkin into a coach. "Well, we'll discuss it. I can be a cover hog."

"You girls will be having a high time," Dad laughs. "Poor Papa will have to room all by himself."

But I know that's not how it will go at all. Instead it will be Dad, Jennifer, and Leelu all teamed up together, and me all on my own. I already had to spend the last couple of weeks watching my best friend slip away from me into enemy camp. I'm not going to let the same thing happen with my sister.

To keep from looking at any of them, I focus on the menu, as though I'm not going to order the same thing I always do when we come here. Still, I'm not sure after this news I'll be able to eat even one bite of my lobster ravioli.

"Daddy, I can go on Space Mountain this time, right?" Leelu asks.

"I think you're big enough now to go on any ride you want," Dad tells her.

"Except not Winnie the Pooh. That's for babies."

"Well, I might want to check it out." Jennifer winks.

Leelu laughs in delight at Jennifer's joke, and starts singing the honey pot song.

"We'll do it if Fiona wants to." Dad's trying to pull me into the conversation.

"But definitely the Haunted Mansion!" The table vibrates with Leelu's uncontrollable bouncing.

"Now that one is my favorite," Jennifer says.

"Yes!" Leelu squeals. "We can go in the same car!"

Which is the last straw. The Haunted Mansion is Cassie's

and my favorite, ever since our families went together two years ago. I've been waiting for Leelu to finally be tall enough, and there's no way I'm going to let Jennifer horn in on that.

In fact, I decide right then and there, I'm not going at all.

Chapter Nine

The idea of not going to Disneyland burns in my mind through the rest of dinner and dessert, but it becomes a flaming bonfire when we do more present opening at home. The rest of the gifts are all things Jennifer got for the Disneyland trip: matching sleep masks, clip-on rhinestoned pouches to keep our money in, and the utter worst—T-shirts. But not just any T-shirts, and not just for me and Leelu.

"IloveitIloveitIloveit!" Leelu gushes, holding hers up for me to see. It's the same as mine, with silver writing on the front that says *I'm a Princess*. On the back are little pictures of Belle, Rapunzel, and all the rest. They're surrounding a special portrait in the middle that's framed just like the others, where somehow there's screened in a picture of Leelu's face. My yearbook picture is in the center of mine.

"Annnnddd . . ." Jennifer reaches into her giant Coach bag. Swirls of pink and silver swim in front of my eyes as she pulls out an identical shirt, with her photo on the back.

"Triplets!" Leelu cheers, pulling hers on straight over her dress.

"Very nice." Dad beams. "Fiona, let's see yours."

"I think I ate too much at dinner," I mumble.

Dad's eyebrows come together. "Are you all right?"

"I just think I need to lie down."

I stand, leaving my gifts on the coffee table. I must look as terrible as I feel, because Dad doesn't even insist I say thank you when I head to my room.

As soon as I'm safe behind my bedroom door, I Face-Time Mom. I'm angry and I'm desperate, and I need immediate, effective action.

"Hello, Fiona," she answers, pushing herself up on her big European pillows so I can see her better. Even though it's Friday night and she's in her pajamas, she has her lap desk spread with a bunch of papers across the bed. She's still working.

"Mom, I can't go to Disneyland." My voice is already starting to shake.

"Oh, Fee. What's all this now?"

"I just don't want to go," I say, as fierce as I can. "Leelu's the one who's excited."

"Is this because of Jennifer?"

A prickle of panic spreads over my skull. Mom's never been anything but polite when it comes to Jennifer, but I don't think she likes her, either. But she and Dad have explained to us a hundred times that we don't always get what we want out of things, and from the way Mom's asking me now I can tell this could turn into one of those situations where I get lectured instead of listened to. I need to use every tactic I can to get out of it.

"It isn't about anything. Except that I changed my mind and I don't. Want. To. Go. Cassie can't go either and it won't be any fun without her. You never asked before if—"

"But Fiona, your father's already made the plans. Everything's reserved. It would be quite an inconvenience for him to undo."

"It's not like we're flying down," I remind her. Which is another reason I can't stand this idea. Watching Leelu and Jennifer pair up over everything at the park will be bad enough, but there's no number of books I could take to help me stomach being stuck in the car with Leelu singing all her favorites alongside someone else. "Dad would only have to cancel my admission, and you know he'll be able to do that, even if it's not allowed."

Mom makes a disappointed face, but she knows I'm right. My father can talk anyone into anything. Except me.

"Please, Mom," I beg. "I can stay with Maritza. I'll do nothing but help around the house. Or the yard, I swear. You won't have to hire Julio."

"You know Maritza's going to visit her family. She timed it for when you and your sister were away."

Desperation pushes at the rims of my eyes in what feel like tears. I hadn't thought about that. "I can come to work with you."

"Fiona, what's gotten into you? You were so excited about this. I understand things with—"

"Leelu will feel so much more grown-up if she gets to go with them by herself," I interrupt. I can't let Mom get me off topic, because then she'll never let me stay home. If I'm going to get out of Disneyland, I have to do it now.

"What if I find something else?" I offer. "Like a camp or something?"

"What kind of camp would possibly still have openings?" Mom sighs, but by the way she's not looking at the camera anymore, I can tell she's already searching. "There aren't a lot of options." Her muttering isn't really to me. "Circus camp?"

I make a face.

"Wilderness adventure—except, no, you're too old. Same with Science Tykes, and"—she sighs again—"Fiona, this is very immature of you. Your father is going to be crushed. Did you think of that?"

But I'm online and searching too, on the school website that lists all the programs we heard about at a boring assembly near the end of the year.

"Creative Writing Camp for Young People," I read aloud, feeling a rush of relief. I send Mom the link, and we look at the details together: *a two-week-long intensive course for serious young writers interested in story craft and oral presentation, led by a local author and former bookstore owner, Ellen Scott.* Her picture does at least make her look friendly.

The screen glow on Mom's face changes from pink to yellow as she clicks to another page. "I can't believe she's still accepting registrations." Then she grunts. "Probably because it's almost as expensive as yoga camp."

Yoga camp. Which Dad always signs us up for.

She takes off her glasses and looks back at the camera. "You have to speak to your father about this first. And your allowance will go toward paying this tuition."

"But Mom!"

"Fiona Renee, do you want to go to Disneyland or stay home? There are only a few weeks between now and then.

I doubt we'll find something else open that is so appropriate for you. You asked me if you could stay here, and this is my solution. I will sign you up, and keep you home, but that's as far as I'm helping you."

My gratitude for Mom's toughness melts into being paralyzed by her tenacity. I don't want to talk to Dad about anything ever again—not that he would even care since now he's got Jennifer.

"All right." It comes out more as a murmur.

"It's close by, too, luckily," she says. "I don't think we could have invented anything more perfect. All you have to do is clear it with Dad."

I can think of a lot of things more perfect than this summer is turning out to be so far, but I just say, "Great."

"Now is there anything else?"

There are so many other things, but she's already doing this for me, and based on all the catalogs and printed spreadsheets laid out before her, I can see there isn't time for whatever else my answer might involve.

"No, ma'am."

Her face softens. "It's been a hard week, hasn't it?"

She doesn't know the half of it.

"Thank you for helping me find a camp," I say.

"All right. Well, tuckle down and get some sleep now. I'll upload this information into our cloud account so your father can read it if he needs to."

"And we'll talk more Monday, right?"

"Yes, love. We'll talk about it Monday."

She tells me to have fun with Dad and Leelu this weekend, and to sleep tight.

When the call ends, I feel both relieved and also somehow not.

Telling Dad I'm Not Going to Disneyland: A Play
by Fiona Renee Coppleton

[Saturday morning, after the last day of school.
HENRI COPPLETON is at the kitchen table, reading on
his tablet and drinking a glass of grapefruit juice. He is
dressed in his workout clothes, and will be leaving for his
weekly racquetball game soon. FIONA COPPLETON joins
him in her pajamas at the table, knowing she has little time
to seize the moment.]

FIONA: Dad?

HENRI: Yes, blossom.

FIONA: [Hesitating] I changed my mind about
Disneyland.

HENRI: [Looking up from screen in shock] What are
you saying?

FIONA: Well, it's just that—

HENRI: *We've been looking forward to this for months. Leelu is—*

FIONA: *I know, but—*

HENRI: *Is this because of Cassie?*

FIONA: *[Wanting to say: You didn't tell me about Jennifer coming, so I'm not telling you the reason why I don't want to go, either.] A little.*

HENRI: *I know you're disappointed that she can't join us, but you can still have a good time with your old dad, eh?*

FIONA: *[Wanting to say: See? You're not even mentioning me having fun with Leelu, because even you know Jennifer will hog all her attention, too. And you'll be so into it you'll forget all about me. I'll just be there watching the three of you have a blast.] It's just that I found this camp.*

HENRI: *[Checks his phone for the time.] A camp that's better than Disneyland? This you must tell me about.*

FIONA: *[Wanting to say: A torture camp in the jungle would be better than this trip now.] It's a writing camp.*

HENRI: *[Sighs.]*

FIONA: *We're hardly going to any camps this summer, and [hoping this part is true] this is the only week I can go. I learned about it at school. [Crosses her fingers against bad luck for bending the truth.]*

HENRI: And I assume you've spoken with your mother about this already?

FIONA: [Wanting to say: Because you would never let me otherwise.] She said I had to talk to you.

HENRI: [Terse] I will speak to her later. [Pushes back chair, stands.] I'll be back by eleven thirty. We will discuss this more then. [Begins to EXIT LEFT, but turns again to FIONA.] This is highly disappointing.

[FIONA says nothing, and does not watch him go, only kicks the table leg twice in sadness and frustration.]

[FIN]

I'm not sure if that's how plays are really written, or if I have really remembered our conversation exactly. After talking to Dad though, I feel so guilty and conflicted that the second I see my diary sitting there on my desk waiting for me, all the doubt and caution about writing in it drops away.

But looking down at the pages when I finish, I still feel strange. Not just about what I said to Dad, but about writing in these pages at all. It's like coming home to a house where someone's changed all the furniture. Maybe you can still find a way to live there, but it's not quite the same.

In spite of my uneasy feeling, or how we ended things, when Dad gets home from his racquetball game, we don't discuss it any further. Before he heads up to shower, all he says to me is, "Your mother and I talked. I will cancel your ticket," and I spend the rest of the afternoon in my room, reading, to avoid him. During dinner he makes a big deal about trading memories with Leelu about the last time we were there, and looking at the website to see what new attractions they might scope out. Afterward he gives me the silent treatment and plays one of Leelu's video games with her instead.

I tell myself that enduring his sulking is way better than a whole week playing the third wheel at Disneyland with Leelu and Jennifer. It still doesn't feel very good.

I'm lying across my bed, staring down at the floor, feeling like the most friendless girl in the world and wondering how I'm going to survive Dad acting like this, when a Snapchat alert chirps in on my phone.

What are you doing Tuesday? It's Aja, throwing me a lifeline without even knowing it.

I don't know. Why?

I just saw River and Tyrick at the movies!!

Hot embarrassment instantly flushes over me at the sight of Tyrick's name. Does Aja somehow know he's my secret crush? Or is she just excited because she likes River, and Tyrick happened to be with him?

You still want to go shop at Del Monte, right? she asks me before I know how to respond.

Of course.

But she must be typing the next message at the same time because it comes immediately in: **Well they want to meet us there!**

My thumbs freeze in the air above my screen. On the one hand I'm excited, and on the other hand something in me still feels wary. I don't really think Aja's trying to trick me, but the back of my head is still burning from where that pencil hit it in English. I need to make sure.

I suck in a breath, glad at least none of this can get copied to anyone else.

Do you like River? I ask her.

She sends back a stream of hearts, and then, **You like Tyrick too, right?**

Her asking so directly makes me pause again. I have never told anyone about my crush on Tyrick besides Cassie. Having the whole seventh grade know about it (even if they haven't identified him) definitely doesn't count. But if I don't have Cassie anymore, maybe I need someone else.

It's scary but I send it anyway: **Yes.**

It takes forever for her to answer. Long enough for me to start regretting I said anything, but when her response comes in, my lips press up in an involuntary smile.

I thought maybe. Just from, you know. That time with what happened to you. And how you look if he ever is around. I think he likes you too, though. And don't worry, unlike with SOME people, your secret is 4eva safe with me!!

When we finish chatting, there are still a bunch of questions whirling in my mind, and since I've already broken open my diary once today, even if it hasn't felt the same, I grab it and a pen and start writing before I think too much more.

Things I Need to Know Before Meeting Pencil with Aja:
Does it count as a date if we're meeting at the mall with
*   two other people?*
What do I wear?
And what do we talk about?
*   * ~~Sports?~~*
*   * Summer plans*
*   * Writing camp?*
*   * Reading, since we definitely have that in common:*
*   * ~~Favorites in class this year~~*
*   * Favorites in general*
*   * Summer goals*

    * *Rereading: yes or no?*
    * *Books into movies*
  * *Family?*
  * *Trips?*

How do I keep my brain from going on the fritz like it is now before I even see him?

Chapter Ten

The questions about Tyrick stay in my mind, and Dad stays cold and silent before Leelu and I go back to Mom's, but before I know it, Aja's middle sister is dropping us off at the mall Tuesday afternoon. We're early, because Aja wants to get some of our own shopping in before meeting the boys at Dylan's Candy Store. I haven't looked for clothes with anyone other than Cassie or my mom before, and right away I'm surprised at the places Aja knows that I've never considered entering.

"Ooh, Fiona, these would look so good on you." She pulls me into a store of nothing but accessories, and goes straight for a rack of earrings, holding up a long pair that look like a rope made out of silver spikes.

I shake my head. "I'm not sure those are me. They'd work for you, though."

She lifts them to her own ears, considering. "Well, you should think about it. You can be a little plain Jane sometimes, no offense."

Usually when someone says "no offense," they really mean the opposite, but the straightforward, nonjudgmental way Aja does it, I know that's not the case.

I catch my reflection in a small strip of mirror on one of the racks hung with Jennifer-sized necklaces and consider myself: hair tightly smoothed down into a bun, small stud earrings, striped button-down, leggings, flats—the exact kind of outfit Cassie says is stylish without being too flashy. I've never thought about trying anything else, since Cassie has so much fun helping me pick out just the right thing, and is always so on point. Next to Aja in her flowing maxi dress and stacks of ivory bangles, though, maybe it is a little plain Jane.

I remind myself Cassie doesn't care what I wear now anyway, so I don't have to keep dressing the way she likes. Maybe it's time to experiment.

I go over to a wall covered with hats, take down one at random, and turn to Aja. "What about this?"

She wrinkles her nose. "Too big for your face. But here." She hands me a red beret.

When I arrange it properly to the side, she smiles. "Very fab. But I still think you need bigger earrings. In fact, we should go sometime to this shop my sisters adore that has amazing accessories. Plato's Closet?"

I shake my head, not knowing what she's talking about.

"It's this secondhand place, but the stuff they get in is *so* groovy. Like this." She moves over to a rack of flowing scarves and takes one out to drape around my neck.

By the time we leave, thanks to Aja and my wardrobe allotment from Dad, I've got a bag full of new accessories, including three pairs of dangly earrings that aren't too big for my taste, but still meet with Aja's approval. I've even looked up Plato's Closet on my phone, and feel excited about going with her when she's back from Seattle.

Aja wants me to put in one of the new earrings I bought before we meet the boys, but there just isn't enough time. We're almost late as it is.

"I'm telling you, he'll like you better if you make a visual statement," Aja says out of the side of her mouth as we approach. "My sister told me."

But River and Tyrick are already waiting outside the candy store. "Hey," they say to us.

"Hey," we say back.

And then we all look at each other, not saying anything else. I'm waiting to follow Aja's lead, since she seems so smart about this kind of thing, but she just bites the side of her lip. The bold, sassy girl from Reverse Spirit Week and our sleepover seems to have disappeared. It's disorienting.

"So, should we go in?" River finally gestures toward the entrance with his elbow, leaving his hands still in his pockets.

We follow him, gazing around at giant bins of rock candy on a stick, Runts and Skittles by the pound, malt balls big as cake pops, stands of chocolate-drizzled pretzels. The smell of sugar in the air is overwhelming, and the Crayola colors everywhere feel like a circus.

"Do you have a favorite?" Tyrick asks as we move past a roll of candy dots on a spool of paper.

All I can picture are the truffles Dad gets Leelu and me for Valentine's Day from a fancy chocolatier near his office.

"Chocolate?" I say.

Tyrick scrunches his nose and shakes his head. "Sour gummies."

I don't know what to say to this. Gummy candies of any kind are disgusting to me, and now all I can picture is Tyrick holding a big wad of them in a mouth full of chewy sugar and spit.

"Here, see?" he says. We're in front of a tower of clear plastic bins, each one with a different gummy inside: worms, apple rings, sour frogs, fiery cinnamon hearts.

"Pick out what you want to try."

I don't want to try any of them, but Aja and River have caught up to us and at the sight of so many gummy choices, Aja squees like a four-year-old in a room full of cupcakes and kittens.

"The peach rings are the best." She reaches for a plastic bag and a scoop.

This somehow transforms both Tyrick and River from awkward, speechless dummies to boys tumbling over each other to say something next. The three of them start pointing, choosing, and comparing all their favorites, as though the gummy candy wall is suddenly the most fascinating and interesting thing any of them has seen in their lives.

I linger for a while, trying to be engaged, but since I don't have much to add to the conversation, and they hardly notice I'm not saying anything, I let myself wander to the front, where there are trays of hand-dipped truffles on silver and gold doilies. I choose four—two for me, two for Leelu, plus a chocolate frog and a tube of chocolate-covered sunflower seeds—to take home later. They aren't custom princess T-shirts, but I hope Leelu will like them.

"Oh, I was going to get you something," Tyrick says behind me as I finish paying, though he looks more relieved than disappointed. He holds up his bag of neon-colored candy. "Do you want one of these?"

"Thanks, but I think I've got plenty."

He shrugs like it's my loss, and doesn't ask me what I bought. The boy in my English class who read out loud with such a clear voice, who had considerate opinions about Phyllis Wheatley and Gilgamesh, seems to have disappeared.

We stroll as a group around the food court, trying to choose where to have lunch. I'm leaning toward a Mediterranean wrap myself, but Aja can't make up her mind, and River seems more interested in telling gross stories he's heard from his brother who's worked at several different fast food places. But of course Aja and Tyrick are enchanted.

"You know they scrape up all the old brown bits from the hamburger grill and just mix that with canned tomatoes to make the chili."

"Oh God!" Aja cries, like this is both the funniest and most disgusting thing she's ever heard. "I am never going there again."

"Don't even ask me about the milk shakes," River adds conspiratorially. "That stuff isn't even milk."

Everyone knows that, I want to say. *It's why my parents never take us there*. But even in my head it sounds snotty.

"Let's just get a slice," Tyrick says, indicating the Sbarro. "At least we know that's safe."

"Well, except for the pepperoni." In my mind it's a joke connected to River's gross-out a minute ago about breakfast sausage, but Tyrick looks at me like I'm from another planet.

"You don't like pepperoni, either?"

Of course I don't, I want to say. At least not pooling with grease, on top of cheap pizza made with canned sauce and plastic cheese, stuck under a heat lamp until someone orders it. But I don't need the weird look he's giving me to know I shouldn't say something like that out loud.

The gross-out conversation doesn't stop when we have our food, either. To take it to an even more foul level, Aja starts telling River about some icky video, and he counters it with another. They're doing everything they can to out-revolt each other, making it hard to choke down my slice of mushroom and cheese. Tyrick isn't any help either, since he seems as entranced with Aja's tales as River is.

It isn't just the conversation that bothers me, though, or that the up-close version of Tyrick is far less interesting than the Pencil I've admired from afar. Sitting there, doing my best to pretend to pay attention, I can't help thinking that if Tyrick and I were spending the afternoon with Cassie and Cory, everything would be going much differently. We would've talked about books and trips or something else I wasn't able to think of in my diary the other day but Cassie would, and there's no way Cassie would have tolerated anything gross (especially having to do with food). She also would've seen how I'm struggling to connect with Tyrick, and would ask good questions to help get us talking, instead of being carried away with her own fun.

"What do you think, Fiona?" Aja says, pulling me out of my stew.

"About?"

"Seeing a movie next?" River says, sliding his eyes at Aja.

"Oh, I don't know." I reflexively hold my hand to my stomach. "I'm not sure I'm feeling that well."

Aja's brow furrows in concern—the real, tender kind she gives Evie. The kind I've wanted from her way before now. "Are you okay?"

"Maybe walking around a little more will help," I say. I don't want to cut short the afternoon, but the idea of waiting around with them for a movie to start, and then sitting there in the dark with Tyrick not knowing what to do, and not being able to ask Aja about any of it, makes me feel queasy for real.

"No, you do look weird," Aja says. "I'll call Jonesy to get us. We can go relax by the pool or something."

"Give me your number," River says to Aja when her sister arrives.

"Yeah." Tyrick turns to me, and I can tell it wouldn't have occurred to him to ask if River hadn't said something. When he finishes typing it in he looks up, straight into my eyes with those golden ones of his, but they don't hypnotize me now. "I hope you feel better."

We say good-bye, and as soon as we're in the car, Aja giggles with delight, and starts telling her sister all the details.

"Ooh, he likes you," Jonesy says when Aja finishes narrating.

"Tyrick likes Fiona too, you can tell." Aja looks at me happily for affirmation.

I try to smile, and say something like, "Yeah," though to be honest I'm not sure I like him anymore. And even though I can't pinpoint exactly why, that feels like something else that's Cassie's fault, too.

Chapter Eleven

Almost the second after Jonesy drops me at Mom's from the mall, Aja texts **OMG SO FUN TODAY THANK YOU SWEETIE YOU ARE THE BEST!! T + F & A + R 4EVA. FEEL BETTER OKAY??? I'LL MISS YOU WHILE I'M ON VACAY!! <3 <3 <3 <3**

It's sweet but also disappointing—she obviously didn't notice how disastrous the outing was for me.

A second message, from Tyrick, makes knowing how to feel even harder:

Dear Fiona. Sorry you feel bad. Hope River wasn't too disgusting. He and Aja still want to catch a movie when she gets back. You want to come too?

I need to get my things together before Maritza takes us over to Mom's, but first I think I need my diary.

> *Pencil, Revised: A Vocabulary List*
> *In Person:*
>> *Confusing*
>> *Perplexing*
>> ~~*Disingenuine (??)*~~ *Uncertain?*
>> ~~*Mundane Average Surprisingly*~~ *Disappointingly*
> *Normal*
>> *Plebian*
>> *And Yet, in His Text:*
>> *Polite*
>> *Thoughtful*
>> ~~*Hopeful? Expectant (??)*~~
>> *Interested*

It's frustrating, not being able to articulate exactly how I feel, especially since I still don't trust putting everything down on the page. I keep stopping to look at Tyrick's text again. And again, and again. I'm flopped on the couch, still staring, when Mom walks past with a stack of folded towels and gets a glance at my screen. "Who's that?"

"The boy I told you about," I admit.

"Everything okay?"

"I think so." But even I can hear how unconvincing I am. The thing I haven't said to Mom, and couldn't put in my diary either, is that I'm wondering if Tyrick somehow actually knows about the Pencil thing, and is only being nice because he feels sorry for me.

Mom glances at Leelu, and when she sees she's engrossed in her iPad, she jerks her head in the direction of the stairs up to the loft that's her room. "I need to put these towels up and then do my stretches."

Mom's stretch time is always a good opportunity for talking, so I follow her upstairs and lie across her pillowy bed. I hand her my phone so she can see. "I just don't know what it means."

"It means he wants to see you," she says, reading. "He's very polite, I think."

"Maybe. But don't you think it's more about River and Aja? She practically forgot I was there as soon as we met them. It feels like he might like her more than me, too. He hasn't said anything else since I texted him back yes."

Mom sits on the floor and extends her legs in a wide V. "There are lots of reasons why someone may not respond immediately. And perhaps Tyrick's more comfortable in a group setting. Which is a good thing, yes?"

She means it's good if he likes group settings, because I'm not allowed to go on a real date—one-on-one with no parents anywhere—until I'm fifteen, and even then I'll have a curfew and he'll be required to meet my parents and give them his cell phone number first. Those are rules Mom and Dad made up before I was even born.

I rest my chin on my hands. "But, Mommy, I'm not even sure I like him anymore. I mean, I think I liked liking him more than actually being with him." *Or when Cassie was around to make a game of the whole thing*, I think but don't say.

"You had a rough first encounter," she says, raising her arms over her head and letting out a long breath. "Some things need time to grow."

"But I'm only in seventh—I mean eighth—grade. I don't need a boyfriend."

"Who says boyfriend?" She chuckles, bending her torso over her outstretched knee. "I'm not rushing boyfriend."

"Then why do you want me to go out with him again?"

She straightens up to look at me. "Fiona, I'm just saying you've made some new friends, they want to see you, and maybe even if everything isn't completely perfect right away, that doesn't mean it will always be a disaster. Not every relationship falls magically into place on the first day of camp the way it did for you and Cassie. Maybe you need to give them another chance."

By the pointed way Mom's looking at me, I suddenly

know she knows what happened with Cassie. Maybe not all the details about my diary, and Kendra, and everything else, but somehow even without my ever figuring out how to tell her, she definitely understands that Cassie and I are in a fight, or not friends, or whatever we are, and more than that, she knows I'm unsure how to talk about it. It dawns on me that probably she and Serena have discussed it, which makes me feel embarrassed, and guilty. Suddenly I *do* want to try to tell her.

"It's probably a phase, anyway," she says, moving on from the topic. "You may simply need to be the friend who can wait it out with her."

I'm not sure if she's talking about Cassie or Aja, but I do know if my upcoming movie outing is going to be anything like today, I'm not sure I can wait in that case. But Mom's mention of Cassie—and her silent reminder that we're not friends anymore—provides me the final good reason I need to give Aja, and Tyrick, a chance.

Because Cassie would die of jealousy if she knew I went out *twice* with my dream crush, while the only boys she has access to now are Gates Morrill and his jerk friends.

After some excited messaging, plus a boring week of yoga camp later, Aja's back in town, and we're standing together scanning the movie theater parking lot for Tyrick and River.

"It's too bad Evie couldn't come," I say. Which is true. Evie was going to be my insurance in case things went poorly with Tyrick again, but she's at a play her parents bought tickets for way before school got out.

"Yeah," Aja says, shrugging, "but you know how Evie's parents are about boys."

I don't know. "About boys?"

"That she can't hang out with them," Aja says simply, before letting out a quiet squeak at the sight of River and Tyrick getting out of a car at the curb. I'm still confused, but River lifts a hand in hello to us both, so I wave back with Aja. Tyrick stuffs his hands in his pockets and looks off to the side, hiding what looks like an embarrassed smile.

"Hey," they say to us, just like at the mall.

"Hey." Aja curls her fingers in a little wave to River.

"Did you have a good trip?" Tyrick asks her.

Aja immediately starts telling stories about Seattle, her cousins, the shows she saw, and the cool shopping she did while she was there. Her stories are good, and I'm glad to hear full details about what she was up to, but the whole time she doesn't ask any of us what we've done, which means there's no chance for me or Tyrick to talk to each other. The dread feeling I had about this outing creeps up again, and I almost consider another fake stomachache. We each pay for our tickets, but Aja keeps steamrolling the conversation right into the Girls Rock camp she's started this week. Tyrick ends up paying for her Sno-Caps, because she's so distracted showing River the calluses on her fingers from playing guitar.

"That was nice of you," I tell him as we walk into the theater. If we're going to say anything to each other, this has to be the time.

He shrugs, embarrassed. I try to keep in mind what Mom said about his being shy, instead of thinking he doesn't want to talk to me. "So what have you been up to so far this summer?"

"Eh. Basketball. Reading some." He looks at River to listen to what he's saying back to Aja.

It's frustrating, and almost makes me believe he somehow *does* know about the Pencil thing, even though up to now I felt sure no one had figured it out. Still, I have no explanation for why he's acting like this, and no desire anymore to try and turn it around.

When the lights begin to dim and the commercials start, I'm more relieved than disappointed.

Broken Pencil

Every day my eyes followed you,
watched you from afar,

wanting to know the depths
of all your secrets.
Your golden eyes
your rich voice
were portals, I was sure,
to complex caverns
inside you that I wanted to know.
Now, close up,
I can see
Your eyes are only eyes.
Your voice only a voice,
without anything interesting to carry it.
Before, you were a puzzle
I so badly wanted to solve,
and now the only puzzle
is wondering
whether it was really you I liked
or if I just liked liking you instead.

I'm out of practice writing poems, and the lines at the end are particularly clunky even if they're more honest. I'm sitting at my desk after the movies, trying to think of how to fix it, when a message from Evie comes in.

So sorry I couldn't go today. The play was good though! I think I want to be an actress now. Or a director. I can't

decide. Anyway, how was it?

I send a mix of emojis that mean I don't know.

????

I don't know if I'll go again.

Why not?

I glance back at my poem. Mom's words about giving new friends a chance are still in my mind, and Evie's been nothing but sweet so far. Maybe she's the one I can lean on.

I think I just liked him better before.

Did you talk to Aja about it? she writes back.

I snort. While I'm glad that she and River are hitting it off so well, and Aja's confidence really is inspiring (instead of annoying like Kendra's), I don't know how to tell Evie that I'm starting to believe the only reason Aja wanted me there was to make it a group thing so she'd be allowed to see River.

But maybe Evie would understand better than I think, especially if what Aja said about her not being allowed to hang out with boys is true.

While my thumbs are hovering over the keys, trying to formulate my exact question, **WHAT DO YOU MEAN YOU DON'T LIKE TYRICK ANYMORE?** comes in from Aja.

I didn't say that, I text back, startled.

EVIE SAYS YOU DON'T KNOW WHETHER YOU LIKE HIM OR NOT.

For a moment I'm not sure what I'm reading. Evie already told Aja?

She misunderstood, I finally send.

WELL??? comes back from her.

I feel cornered. **We just don't talk much.**

IS THAT ALL HIS FAULT?

It's way too harsh of her to say, especially when she's the one who hogs all the conversation.

It's SOMEbody's, I slam back.

Hope that means you know it's you.

It's infuriating. Aja's straightforwardness has been so appealing in the past, but this is taking it too far. **I thought you were supposed to be my friend.**

Friends say things straight, she answers.

If this is how Aja really is, I don't care what Mom says. I'm not giving her any more chances. **Maybe I don't want you to say anything to me for a little while.**

But there *is* still one thing I want to know right this minute from Evie, so I switch over to our chat. **Why did you tell Aja?** I challenge her.

She gives good advice. I wanted to help you feel better.

Well you only made things worse, I send hotly back. She should have known Aja would overreact, since the two of them are best friends.

I'm staring at the screen waiting for either of them to respond when a message from Tyrick appears: **Aja says you don't want to hang anymore I guess. Sorry about that. Have a nice summer.**

It makes me so mad I throw my phone, hard, onto the carpet. I never should have trusted two girls I barely know, even if they both seemed so great at the beginning. I should've learned from Cassie that no matter how close you are, a friend can turn on you at any moment.

Chapter Twelve

To avoid any reminder of Aja, Evie, Tyrick, or the fact that now I have no friends at all, I keep my phone in the nightstand drawer, and keep away from any tablets or laptops. Which means there's nothing much to do the next day except stay out of the way while Leelu and Maritza spend the entire afternoon doing laundry and packing her up for Disneyland tomorrow. I'm trying to watch TV, since I read most of the morning, but it's nearly impossible with my sister doing Ariel and Olaf impersonations—loudly, and obnoxiously, on purpose, from the other room—no matter how many times I holler at her to quit.

"Leelu, I can't hear what's on!" I scream at her from the couch for the six-thousandth time.

"What?" she singsongs from our room.

"You heard what I said."

She comes out to the living room to look at me.

"What?" I say again when she stays bug-eyed and silent.

Her face twists into a prissy sneer. "You're just jealous."

She hasn't been this mean to me in a long time. I'm shocked, but I guess now that she has a twinkly new partner in Jennifer, she doesn't need to be nice to me anymore.

"Nope, I can't wait for you to leave."

"Girls, girls," Maritza says, bringing in another basket of laundry from the garage.

"Enough of this snitting. Leelu, did you finish sorting all your shoes or not? We cannot make choices until you know where all of them are. Hurry, hurry. Your mama will be home soon and there is dinner yet and washing your hair."

I hear Leelu saying her hair doesn't need washing since Dad took her to the parlor to have it rebraided this week, but Maritza apparently doesn't agree. I'm not four minutes back into my show before she starts up again, this time a genie song from *Aladdin*.

Which does it. I stomp down the hall, still holding the remote.

"Not everything is about Disney all the time, okay?" I holler at her. "You're going to be there in twenty-four hours, so can you bottle it up and—"

I stop midsentence, shocked. Our room is a disaster. Even though Leelu and Maritza have been packing for what feels like hours, nothing has actually made it into a suitcase. The floor is spread out with every single shoe Leelu owns, and my desk is crowded with her activity books, art supplies, and all the other things that will go into her backpack. Both of our beds are still covered with outfits, with her matching stuff from Jennifer right on top—of, what I realize, are the Mickey sweat shorts and *Monsters, Inc.* shirt I got signed by some Pixar animators last time we went.

I snatch my stuff off her bed, not caring that her eye mask from Jennifer falls to the mess on the floor. "When were you going to ask if you could take these, huh? You don't have my permission."

She crosses her arms. "Well, you're not going to wear them."

"They're my things!"

A whine crawls into her voice. "You wouldn't even know I had them if you hadn't come back here."

"I wouldn't have had to come back here if it weren't for your stupid singing!"

"Girls, enough," Maritza scolds us both. "Leelu, give those back. Shame on you, sneaking. I don't like it when you lie to me, and you're not supposed to take things from your sister without asking."

The alarm at the front door beeps. "Hello?" Mom calls.

Immediately Leelu bursts into tears and goes running to her. Maritza makes a frustrated noise and tosses her hands up, before Mom appears in the doorway with Leelu pressing her wet face into her hip. I feel bad about making Leelu cry, but she didn't have to rub it in my face that she doesn't care about me anymore by going and stealing my stuff.

"Leelu, what is this?" Mom says with frustration.

"She's a liar and a thief," I tell Mom.

"Am not!" Leelu shouts.

"She took my things without asking and told Maritza they were hers."

"Did not!"

"Did so!"

"Did NOT!" Leelu screams.

"Fiona, upstairs to my room immediately. You're not budging until we talk. Leelu, you need to get this mess cleaned up this minute and get your suitcase packed. I'll talk to Maritza, and when I come back in here I better see some real progress."

"But Mom—" we both say at the same time.

She raises a finger, nostrils flaring wide. "I'm not repeating myself. Please do as I ask."

I grab my diary, my pen, and my latest library book off the table between our beds, making a big show of how difficult it is to step over all of Leelu's stuff. Mom says my name in a low warning, but it's Leelu who's wrong, not me. I stomp up the stairs, pleased with the loud smacks my feet make on the tile, shutting out the sound of Leelu's wailing. I had actually started to feel sad about missing this vacation with her and Dad, but now I can't wait for him to get her out of my sight.

Mom says sleeping on something always makes it better, but she's wrong because in the morning there's Dad picking Leelu up, with Jennifer sitting in the front seat. I want to hug Leelu close, and beg her not to love Jennifer more than me, but she just skips past without a care, pulling her My Little Pony suitcase behind her like it's magically turned into a real prancing horse. It doesn't matter if I apologize; she's not even in the car yet and my fears have already come true.

Dad hugs me and asks again if I'm sure I won't change my mind, but I can barely hug him back. No way am I going now, no matter how conflicted I feel about it.

As they drive away, Mom and I stand in our little yard and wave, but I don't keep my hand up very long.

"Sweetheart, I'm sorry, but I've got to get moving," Mom says, checking her phone.

"But it's Saturday. And Maritza's not here yet."

"You know this is my busy season, darling, and she's not coming, remember? Since you were both supposed to leave today, she's getting ready for her own trip."

I'd forgotten. "But what am I supposed to do?"

"Well, let's see. How about: Read. Watch movies. Dance. Write. Draw. Clean. Dust. Take a bath. Start a project. Research someone interesting in history. Organize your photos into files. . . ."

She's making fun of me. "No one's going to be here, though."

"Fiona, you're twelve years old. You have a cell phone, and you know Mrs. Carroll right next door, plus the Tandigens in the building across the parking lot. There's plenty in the pantry for you to eat, and you can make grilled cheese if you want. I trust you're not going to set the house on fire. You're still not quite old enough to look after your sister alone, but for one day, over the summer, I thought you would be pleased."

"I—" Ordinarily, I would be grateful, but right now it just sounds lonely.

"I'll be home by six thirty and we can go out for dinner, since we didn't make it last night. In fact, let me set a reminder to make a new reservation."

Mom goes to get ready, leaving me—for what will be the entire day—to my own devices.

•   •   •

It turns out, even when your sister's turned on you, when you're kind of in a fight with all your new friends, and you totally hate your old best friend for destroying your life and your summer, being by yourself all day can be pretty boring.

Attending your mom's boss's Fourth of July pre-celebration the next day is also boring (even if there's a giant pool, more hot dogs than I've ever seen in my life, and a huge sheet cake decorated with strawberries and blueberries like the American flag), because none of those things are much fun when there aren't any other kids to talk to. Evie does send me a message filled with little firework emojis Monday morning, which feels like a truce, but it doesn't make me forgive her all the way for butting in about Tyrick, especially since Aja hasn't said another word to me. I would try to check my feed to see if she's posted anything lately, but then I'd run into something of Cassie's, so I spend most of the party curled in a corner with another library book.

Since Mom has the holiday off, we go grocery shopping and run a bunch of other errands, including taking time to get pedicures together at a spa we know will be open. It's a surprising treat in general, but especially without Leelu around, because she *always* wants pedicures.

"Leelu will be jealous," I say to Mom as we choose our polish.

"Well, she'll get plenty of the princess treatment where she's going."

Her mock-exasperated tone feels like a private joke between us, and I lean a bit into her, enjoying the closeness. She puts her arm around me and we twirl the rack slowly, taking our time choosing the right color—another thing we can't do with Leelu around, since she always grabs iridescent pink right away.

"My sisters and I used to fight right before one of us was going away on a trip, too," Mom tells me after a minute.

I look up at her.

"When you love each other so much, it's hard being apart."

"She hates me." I suddenly feel sad. "Everyone does."

"Leelu doesn't hate you. I bet she misses you right this minute. And you have Aja, and Evie, too."

Probably both of us notice she doesn't mention Cassie. It's surprising that she still hasn't, and disappointing in a way I can't quite describe. At the same time, though, it also feels grown-up. Like she trusts I'll come to her when I'm ready to.

"Aja's mad because I don't like Tyrick anymore," I admit.

Mom's face is half curious, half amused. "I have a feeling she'll get over that. Besides, you're the one who decides who you like, not her. Just listen to yourself."

It'd do no good to point out that *Cassie* apparently hasn't gotten over anything, or how hard it is to listen to yourself when everyone else abandons you. Maybe they're right, instead of Mom.

"It's a good thing you're starting that new camp tomorrow," Mom says after we're settled in our chairs and I still haven't responded. "This class could be the fresh start you need."

I don't want to think about camp yet. I want it to be just me and Mom, like this, for a while. But as soon as I sink my feet into the warm, bubbling water, my phone jangles in my purse with a FaceTime call.

Mom indicates I should answer it. "It's probably your sister."

"Hi, sissie." Leelu waves into the camera when I get it turned on.

Dad leans in. "We miss you, Fiona."

Seeing both of them makes me miss them immediately too, until the screen jiggles and shifts, and Jennifer's face appears. "Could you believe those fireworks last night, Fee?"

I dismiss her with an "mmm" noise. The truth is, I

could hardly watch the video she sent of Leelu prettily waving sparklers at the night parade and gazing at the overwhelmingly beautiful fireworks, because it made me too sad. Tonight's official Fourth of July show will be even more extravagant.

"Look what Jennifer got me." Leelu brings the phone closer to her chest, where she's holding out an aquamarine snowflake pendant on a thin silver chain: something much prettier and more sophisticated than the Elsa junk I was certain she'd come back with. "And there's a ring too, see?"

She moves her hand so close to the camera that the ring is too blurry, but it shines with just as many rhinestones as the pendant. My sadness hardens into something tight in my throat. Leelu's not worried about our fight anymore, but only because of something terrific Jennifer did.

"We have one picked out for you too," Dad says. "Leelu just couldn't decide what color."

"I don't need one," I say.

Leelu frowns. "But then we'll match."

"I have enough jewelry." I make sure Jennifer hears it too.

Dad chuckles. "We will pick you out something else, then. There are still plenty of days, and so much we haven't seen."

Leelu interrupts, so Dad doesn't hear me telling him pictures will be fine.

"Me and Jennifer have our own suite! There are fluffy robes, and slippers, and a whole couch for each of us. Plus enough pillows for a giant pillow fight, not even counting the ones on the beds. We went on Ariel's carousel three times in a row just because we can, and tomorrow we're making cartoons at the Animation Academy!"

Saying "just because we can" is a totally Jennifer thing, and I wonder if she taught it to my sister while they were having their giggly pillow fight on their magical sleepover. Mom jumps in to ask if Dad can send a copy of Leelu's cartoon when she's done, so I don't have to say anything, which is good because all I can do is picture a Snow White remake, starring Jennifer as the pretty queen transformed into a horrible witch. Or maybe the one who lures children into her candy house and then gobbles them up for her dinner.

It'd be a great first thing, I realize, to write tomorrow in creative writing camp.

Chapter Thirteen

Even through my gloom about Leelu, and nervousness about a new class, Mom's words about a fresh start come back to me the next morning. Camp won't simply be a place where I can write whatever mean stories about Jennifer I want—I'll also be anonymous. The kids enrolled are from schools all over. Nobody will have any idea who I am, or, more importantly, who my former best (jerk) friend is and what happened with my diary.

I hop out of bed and open up my side of the closet. If everything in my life has to start completely over, maybe I should look the part, too.

Even with the help of the accessories Aja and I got, admittedly there's not much in my wardrobe that isn't plain

Jane. Most of it is leggings, jeans, and tops that Cassie helped me pick out, and I definitely don't want to wear any of that. As I push farther back in my closet, I find a wrap-around skirt with big splashy poppies on it. When I opened it on my eleventh birthday (a present from Tante Juno, my aunt), Cassie wrinkled her nose at the blotchy floral print. I pull it out, knowing it's perfect, even if none of my Cassie-approved tops will work with it. But on Leelu's side I find an old black leotard that still fits. I wrap the silver paisley scarf I bought with Aja around my neck to dress it up a little. Flats will have to do, but at least the rest is different.

At the last minute I find the red beret and pull it over my still sleeked-down hair. And, for good measure, I grab the butterfly-covered journal I got from my grandparents last birthday. Writing these new entries in my diary has felt okay, but if this is going to be a fresh start, I want it to be a real one.

"Oh, I love that skirt," Mom says when I meet her in the kitchen. "You haven't worn it much, have you? And the beret is new. I like it."

The warmth of Mom's approval, and the small shred of confidence I can cling to in my new outfit, disappear the moment we walk into the upper-floor classroom at the library, though. Inside, there are six kids already waiting—two boys and four girls—all of them wearing T-shirts, flip-flops, and shorts.

I look ridiculous.

But the woman I recognize as our teacher glances up and smiles. "Good morning." She has pale, pale skin covered in freckles, and is wearing a faded yellow sundress with an orange cardigan over it, so at least I'm not the only colorful one.

We say good morning back and Mom shakes her hand, before asking if Ellen's read the note that says I have permission to stay in the library after the workshop is over until she comes to get me at four.

"Everything's in order," Ellen tells Mom. "And I'd be worried about you, Fiona, staying after late, except I spent most of my summers hanging out at the library too, and it worked out pretty well for me."

I nod. Up close Ellen's eyelashes are white blond, and there's a big, single freckle perched right on the ridge of her upper lip. When she smiles again at me she looks like a bright, happy daisy, and I decide I like her.

"Sit wherever you like." She gestures to the table where the other kids are. "We're just waiting on a few of the others."

I look at Mom, suddenly not wanting her to leave. She doesn't like the idea of me hanging out in the library for so long after class either, but since Julio's counseling at a camp back east, it's the best option until next week when

Maritza is back. It'd be embarrassing to look worried or be too kissy in front of other kids, so I squeeze her hand and show her in my eyes that I will be okay.

Once she's gone, I take in the rest of the table. One girl is busy drawing what looks like anime dragons all over the inside cover of her notebook, and another is deeply engrossed in a book in her lap that I can't see but immediately want to. Two more girls with glasses and braces sit at the farthest corner, snuffling with giggles over some game on their phones. The boys are on opposite ends of the table, with the giggling twins and our teacher, Ellen, in between. The bigger, taller one is staring fixedly at a single spot on the ceiling, like if he concentrates hard enough he'll make the whole room disappear. But the other, smaller one, with long black curls mopped all around his face and neck, is looking straight at me. When our eyes meet, he points with his pen, smiles, and says, "I like your skirt."

I smile in thanks and sink into the nearest chair across from him, right as the rest of the students and their parents pour in. One of the moms apologizes about a problem with the elevator in a way that's really a complaint, but Ellen greets each parent and student with a handshake and her relaxed smile. It gives the rest of us a chance to check each other out. There are two more boys in the group (obviously friends who signed up together), and three more girls, the last of whom stands out to me in part because of the big rhinestone flower she has pinned in her smooth and tight Afro, but also because she's the only other black girl in the whole group. As I suspected when Mom and I looked at the other registrations, I don't know anyone from school, so at least that's good.

Fresh start, I remind myself, smoothing my skirt for reassurance.

"Welcome to creative writing camp," Ellen says once everyone's seated and the parents are gone. "I'm looking forward to working with all of you. But since this is a writing class, before we do anything else, let's take out our materials and get warmed up."

I can tell by the hesitant looks going around the table that most of us were expecting at least a name game first, but we take out our tools anyway. On our errands yesterday, Mom bought me a new assortment of pens and pencils—including a new sharpener—and a vinyl pencil case to zip them all up in. It's tidy, and sophisticated I think, but to my surprise I'm almost the only one using paper and pencil; several kids have tablets or laptops with them, just like at school.

"One thing we tend to do as writers," Ellen tells us, "is edit ourselves before we put down the first word. How many of you have gotten an idea for a story, and then told yourself 'Oh no, that's stupid,' before you've even started writing?"

There are several shy sounds of confirmation, and the two girls who were playing on their phones before nudge each other.

"It's very important to get comfortable with *not* doing that," Ellen says. She explains about first thoughts and how necessary it is to get them down, without any editing or censoring. "That can come later. You can always revise. At first, perhaps what you write will be nonsense, but I promise you, it's only by writing through all that that the good stuff comes out."

She tells us she'll give us a prompt, and then it's very important to write whatever comes to mind—no matter how silly it is—and keep going until she tells us to stop.

The girl with the sparkling flower in her hair raises her hand. "What if you can't think of anything else?" she asks.

"Write whatever's in your head next," Ellen says. "Let your mind go, and your pen will follow, I promise."

I glance across the table. The boy with the curls and I trade uncertain looks, and I can tell he knows as well as I do that good writing isn't all over the place—it's tight and careful and thoughtfully constructed.

"All right, gang," Ellen says. "Your first word is 'summer.' Write anything and everything that comes to your mind about the word 'summer,' until time's up."

Summer, I write at the top of the first page in my stiff new journal.

> *Beach time. Play time. Friend time. Pool time. No more pencils no more books no more Izzy Gathing dirty looks.*

I smile at that, but keep writing as instructed.

> *Sunburn. Sunshine. Bathing suits. Parties. Grilling. Sailboats. Hammock naps. Everyone outside and having a good time. Friends together playing singing laughing shouting running: no one around to take away their fun—pure happiness spinning in the sand without a care, forgetting the pressures of school and friends and new girlfriends and broken families and everything else. Only you and me sunning and playing and laughing, everything healed and nothing between us broken.*

Right when I'm getting into it, Ellen tells us it's time to stop. I stare at my paper, feeling loopy, dazed, and disappointed it's over. By the looks of everyone else around the table, it doesn't seem I'm alone.

"We'll be doing that again," Ellen says, proud of us, "but now that we've tried that out, let's get to know each other."

The game Ellen uses for us to learn each other's names is one I've played before: picking a descriptive word that begins with the same letter as our first name, and putting that word in front when we introduce ourselves.

"For example, I'm Effervescent Ellen."

Each time a new person says his or her name, we go back around the circle repeating everyone's who has come before. This is how I learn Galactic Grace (the girl drawing all the dragons), Cool Connor, Jellyfish Julian, and Mercury Michael (who was looking at the ceiling before like he wanted to disappear). Then Meridian and Megan, the identically dressed girls on the corner who are apparently not related (though they both choose Marshmallow for their word), and eXacting Xi (the girl with the book I still can't see). Ridiculous Ruby, Adventurous Austen, and, next to me, Dynamic Diamond, who pushes her teeth forward in a gigantic smile and tosses her hands wide when she says her name, reminding me a little of Aja. The black-haired boy who complimented my skirt introduces himself as "Sideways Sanders."

Everyone has such surprising words, I start to feel doubtful. Usually I just say "Friendly," but now that seems too boring. "Fantastic" might be show-offy, but "Fun" is too obvious. I'm not sure what to pick, until what Ellen said, about not editing yourself before you write anything down, pops into my head.

"Fearless Fiona," I say when it's my turn, surprising myself. I'm not sure it's really true, but I suppose I'd like it if it could be. The smiles of approval Sideways Sanders and eXacting Xi give me from across the table help me think that it might.

Ellen's freewriting trick works the rest of the morning, too. I had no idea how much could come out of a couple of easy prompts, once you stop worrying what it's going to look like at first. After a couple more sessions like this, we move on to revising, but having so much material to work with makes it heaps easier to shape a piece. Ellen gives us some exercises that help us refine first thoughts into a mini essay, and at the end of the day, we share. Some of the stories are funny, like Grace's about her irrational fear of beach balls when she was little, but then Austen reads one about the summer her new baby half sister was born. Seeing how creative and free everyone can be, including myself, only makes me want to do more of this exact kind of thing.

It helps too that everyone is so friendly, and into the writing. Even Michael got over the anxiety he seemed to be feeling at first by lunchtime, asking Grace to show us her dragon illustrations. It inspired me to ask Xi about the book she was reading before class (I'm Fearless Fiona after all), and when she showed me a fantasy novel I'd never heard of, Austen jumped in to tell me how good it is. The three of us got into a rapid-fire book-recommending spree that eventually absorbed the whole group, and there were so many titles flying around that I didn't feel awkward at all about mentioning a dusty classic like *Little Women*.

By the end of the day, when I'm waiting for Mom in the library, I can't wait to tell her how right she was about that fresh start.

Chapter Fourteen

Things I Love About Writing Class:
    Ellen's smile
    Grace's drawings
    Diamond's dramatic readings
    The way Michael half chokes when he laughs
    Freewriting, freewriting, freewriting
    Sharing ideas
    Making new friends
    Exploring everything
    —see, even this doesn't feel enough, now that I know
what it's really like to keep the pen going, going, going
putting anything and everything down to keep or discard
as I wish, not needing everything to be so tidy and smart

*like in my old diary trying to perfectly record every
single thought and moment, or then after when I wanted
everything shrunk down and minimal. Thoughts aren't
trapped or finite! And they don't have to be restricted!
They are fluid and malleable and you can make them from
something raw into something more shareable, if you want,
or they can stay that way, leaving an interesting trail for
you to follow later. The early stuff that comes out—that
isn't for everyone, like Ellen says, and I know that all
too well, but it doesn't have to define you, either. I know
I've always loved writing, but before I spent so much
time worrying about vocabulary and trying to develop
structure. I was always focusing on how it looked, and
even though I was putting down my thoughts—even before
the Incident—they were only half bits of what I truly feel.
They were one side instead of all sides. Linear instead of
upsidedownbackwardwhateveryouwant. Before, I was so
careful with my writing but look what happened! I still
got made fun of. Now I have this class and Ellen and my
friends and no one flinches if I write something like Aja
is a parade of herself with her own mouth the marching
band. That doesn't even make sense, and it's not wholly
true (though I still haven't heard from her). Maybe I was
a piccolo in that parade marching behind her too. See?*

I can say stuff like that! Or, this: Evie sweetie pie cute curly button beauty with a dimply smile treating people so fragile they break in her fingers, turning to porcelain doll pieces on the floor when all she wanted was to play. It's how I feel, sort of, but also there's this: Evie wrapping bandages around burns—Florence Nightingale to the rest of us, how your messages are a balm to me, a lost soldier of so much war tired of fighting so yes I will put down my weapons and answer you.

Again, I don't actually feel like a soldier, but Evie has kept messaging me and sending me pictures, even when I don't say anything back. She's just there, and present, and I can't be mad at her anymore. She avoids the topic of Aja too but at least it's better between us.

And Sanders! So wild funny smart with a seersucker personality in a wolf boy body. Someone who makes me happy to look at but only as a friendly face without that magic hypnotic aura of ~~Pencil~~ Tyrick (SAY IT OUT LOUD IT'S ALREADY OUT THERE). Also Xi chee makes me snee-ze, Leelu lost lingering in the land of the ladies in waiting, waiting to snap up my sweet little sister—my lifeline my only one—and keep her for herself. Because Jennifer knows jewels when she sees them and wants to hoard them all.

I can say these things and on and on and on and on until my hand breaks and I have to rest my eyes but my mind all the time whirling, whirling, whirling.

Pages and pages come out like that. Sometimes in them I'll find a line to start a new essay or poem with, and sometimes I'll even rip out the page (something I would never do to my pretty old diary) and start over. Either way, in class my brain and my eyes and my fingers are all crackling with sparks, and I never want to stop, ever. It's so freeing that on hair-wash day, I decide to let my flyaway curls air dry the way I used to, instead of trying to pin them back. If my writing isn't held down anymore, I don't want the rest of me to be, either.

It all feels so great, and so free, until Thursday.

"Writers, if I may," Ellen says in her polite but commanding way. "Today we're changing things up. You've done so well so far, that now I want you to push yourselves even more."

She explains that for the next two days, we'll be paired with a response partner. Ellen will give us prompts and lessons to help us develop one longer, more intensive project, to be workshopped closely with our partners. Next week we'll write a second story, and on the last day we'll each get to present to the whole group whichever final piece we like best.

Immediately my confidence disappears. Private freewriting has been great, but smaller pieces are my forte, not long fiction stories. I can come up with a good idea to start, but I can never figure out how to keep going. For epic make-believe, it's better if I can work off another person, like Cassie or my sister. Last time I had to write a story for English, Leelu came up with the whole ending. But she's far away, forgetting all about me thanks to Jennifer, and I'm on my own. At least I get paired with Sanders. Maybe he'll be helpful.

"For our first two days you practiced writing outside of your comfort zone," Ellen says when we're settled next to our partners, "but there's always new territory to be explored. Today I want you to think of your favorite kind of story, and write the exact opposite. For example, if you really love fantasy novels, try something historical. Or if realistic fiction is your favorite, insert some dragons."

There are groans of disapproval, especially from Julian and Austen.

"What if you never read anything but graphic novels?" Michael asks, face squinched all over again with anxiety.

"If you have trouble," Ellen assures, "I'll help get you started, but why don't we give it a try? First thoughts is all I want for now. Just put them down. The rest will come." She starts the timer, which means time to stop talking and get to work.

Sanders and I trade "oh well" looks, and I stare at my paper. Writing a whole story is very different from writing whatever you want on the page. It requires a good beginning, a complicated plot, and a satisfying resolution, or else it's not worth reading—which is why I've had so much trouble before. And what's the opposite of what I like, anyway? All my favorite stories are about real girls, facing real problems, like *Little Women* or books that take place now by authors like Jacqueline Woodson or Wendy Mass. I certainly don't know how to write about dragons. Or how to make it any good.

Since Ellen wants us to get down first thoughts, though, I put *What's the Opposite of Real?* on a blank page in my journal.

> *Fantasy*
> *Imaginary*
> *Pretend*
> *Dystopian romance*
> *Horror*

At that last word, a sentence pops into my head: *Callie Harper started out as a nice, smart, pretty, normal girl, until the day she and her friends read from an ancient and powerful book, and Callie became the Haunted.*

It's clunky, and I'm surprised the subject of my horror story isn't immediately Jennifer, but I try not to criticize or question. Maybe going with this story will be as liberating as freewrites.

Her friend Kandra found the mysterious book on a picnic, and decided to read the passages aloud. Neither girl could conceive that the book was protected by a powerful spell ~~that would render whomever~~ that decreed if anyone undeserving read its masterful contents, they would immediately and irrevocably be transformed into a ghost zombie. And anyone within hearing range was doomed by the same fate.

"It's good," Sanders says when he reads my first draft an hour later. "But how come this Kandra reads the book in the first place?"

"Because she's . . . evil."

"I guess I mean, this whole ghost zombie business is strong, but it makes things too complicated. You have to explain why the book has that kind of curse on it. Where it came from. What if, instead of Kandra reading the book out loud, it's Callie who does it? Maybe reading it frees some kind of ghost—Kandra Black—from the book?"

159

It isn't what actually happened, but it does keep me from having to explain a bunch of things that aren't very interesting. "That sounds a lot better. I'll try it."

I give him the best feedback I can on his robot romance, which is almost too funny to really criticize, and we get back to writing.

> *Little did Callie Harper know that on the day she lifted the book from its careful hiding place, and read aloud from its pages, she would become doomed forever to ~~follow the evil commands of~~ serve as a zombie slave to the ghost of the notorious soul-sucker Kandra Black. Kandra was as hungry as she was powerful. Once the final words spilled from Callie's lips, she ceased being the good girl everyone knew her to be, and transformed into a thoughtless minion of her new, long-dead mistress.*

We trade revisions again before lunch, and Sanders tells me this version is much stronger. With his help, I craft a story in which Kandra commands Callie to snatch up the souls of unwitting sixth graders, in order to keep Kandra young and beautiful forever. They join forces with a new corporate recruit, Jenny Malone (who steals not souls but expensive jewelry and other people's children). Jenny funds their mission, making Kandra (and Callie) nearly impossible to defeat.

"Two words for what you need next," Sanders says, when he hands me my pages at the end of the day. "Ninja sword fight."

Those are actually three, and I teasingly say so to Sanders. Mainly, I have no idea how to write a ninja sword fight scene, but he just says, "Get started, anyway. You can always change it later."

So after class is over, I park myself at a desk in the library and keep working, reminding myself to trust whatever comes to mind.

> *Kandra was powerful enough to overtake the likes of Callie and Jenny, but she wasn't smart enough to know that the nearby fire station housed a very special kind of local firefighter—the kind who had long been practicing the ancient ninja arts in order to protect others from dread monsters such as herself.*

I know right away that the fire station idea is lame, and wish I had my sister with me. They're all probably having too good a time in the thick of their Disneyland adventure to even notice if I sent Leelu a message for story crafting help through Dad, though. I'll think of something smarter tomorrow, I tell myself, at least in time to share with class before the weekend.

But writing through the fight scene between Kandra, Callie, Jenny, and the firefighting ninjas only makes things worse, because I have no idea how to describe anything involving blood and guts. I wish I'd traded numbers with Sanders so I could ask him for advice. I can't do this on my own. I need to think the way he would about it.

"Mom, have you seen any ninja movies?" I ask her first thing when she picks me up.

"I can't say many, no. Why?"

I explain our general assignment, and the gist of my story. When I'm finished, she chuckles, low.

"That certainly sounds dramatic."

"I know. But I don't think it's dramatic enough. I mean, I know Ellen wants us to write the opposite of what we usually do, but I think the fight at the end needs to be more realistic."

"Well, I don't know about ninjas, but there's an old movie your Tante Juno likes with some pretty good fight scenes in it. It's too violent for you to watch the whole thing, but with Leelu still gone we could find some clips."

We order pizza and change into pajamas before curling together on the couch so Mom can fast-forward through big chunks of the movie to the best (but still appropriate) parts. She's right—the fights are intense, and I only need to see a few of the girl in the yellow jumpsuit swinging her sword

162

to know exactly what my scenes need. I release Mom to watch whatever she wants, because I've seen enough. Back in my room (after I text Tante that I liked the movie), I'm so focused on my story that when Mom gets a call from Disneyland, I only wave a brief hi. I don't need to hear about Disney Princesses, or even have Cassie to collaborate with anymore. Instead I've got Sideways Sanders and his kung fu masters with a taste for revenge.

"This is great," Sanders says the next morning, laughing. "You make them sound so realistic."

His approval spreads like a cape of confidence across my shoulders.

"But what if"—he looks thoughtful—"instead of being Kandra Black's slave, Callie gets fully possessed by her instead? That way Callie's not even Callie anymore—just Kandra in a different body."

"Ugh," I groan. "I'd have to rewrite the whole thing."

And then this story gets really *far from what happened*, I think too.

"Sometimes you have to write through something before you know what it actually is, right?" He copies Ellen's warm smile perfectly.

And I know he's right. Distancing myself from what happened between me and Cassie (even if only in fiction) is probably better for me anyway. Who cares anymore about the actual diary debacle, or Cassie, and Kendra, or anyone else? This is my story and I can make it into whatever I want.

Iona watched in horror as, below them in the ruins of the chapel, the dread book slipped from Asha's hand.

"No!" Iona screamed, her voice tearing through the dark. "Not you too!" Iona had warned Asha about the book, and Kandra Black, but the temptation to experience Jenny's riches must have been too great.

"It's a shame." The leader of Ninja Fire Squad put her hand on Iona's shoulder. "But she will have to go as well. Are you ready?"

Iona stared down the hill, where Kandra and her gang were gathered in their secret ritual, inducting Asha into their fold. She gripped the handle of the razor-sharp bone knife strapped to her belt. She was afraid to fight, but if it meant freedom from Kandra Black, she knew she would.

There was a blur, a shriek, and before Iona had finished nodding to show her readiness, the Ninja Fire Squad descended down the hill to the ruins, a mass of black and gray—and fury. Iona, lacking their ninja

*training, ran as fast as she could down the hill but still
trailed behind. By the time she reached the ruins, Asha's
eyes—colored the telltale bile yellow that indicated her
zombie status—were rolled back in her head, both legs
severed and spouting blood. Iona was horrified at her
friend's death, but was grateful she hadn't had to witness
her in zombie form.*

*The members of the NFS had taken out the dread Jenny
Malone as well, and as Iona stepped over her blood-soaked
carcass, Iona felt no pity. She joined them at the back of
the ruined sanctuary, where they had cornered Kandra
(still in the form of Callie) and were locked in a grisly and
frightening fight.*

*"You'll never vanquish me!" Kandra/Callie shrieked,
showing teeth that were gray and blackened with rot.
She leaped from where she had climbed atop the altar,
attacking the rear group of the NFS. She fought with
bare hands, her nails grown long and newly sharpened
to deadly claws, but she was no match for the squad. In
a rapid barrage of hand-forged steel and lightning-quick
reflexes, three members seized Kandra/Callie while the
fourth made a clean slice across the ghoul's middle, spilling
her guts to the floor. In spite of the gore and Callie's dying
screams, Iona was not deterred. She gripped the enchanted*

bottle the White Witch had given her atop the mountain,
and murmured the secret activation chant. The bottle
glowed in her hand, pulsing with its ancient power, and
Iona raised her knife, ready to plunge it into the escaping
soul of Kandra Black in the manner she had been taught,
capture it as it fled Callie's body, and bury it with the
proper rites at the bottom of Doom Mountain forever.
Callie would not survive, but at least the world would be
safe from the likes of Kandra Black.

Everyone bursts into applause and cheers of "Awesome" when I read the final version out loud at the end of class, making an uncontrollable smile spring to my face. The hard work I did with Sanders, and the class's praise for it, feels nice, but when I sit back down and it's Austen's turn, I still feel something's wrong with my ending. I haven't been sure about it for days, but hearing it out loud, I know it's still not right.

Camp is over for the week, but while I'm waiting for Mom I take one of the big red armchairs in the library to read my story over with a more critical eye. I comb through line by line, wondering if it's the descriptions that are unsatisfying. Around me people walk back and forth, browsing shelves and checking out books, so I don't look up when one seems to be coming in my direction. Not until they're standing right over me, unavoidable.

Kendra Mack.

"Oh, hi, Fiona," she says, like we just ran into each other by accident, instead of her walking purposefully all the way over here to talk to me. "What are you doing here?"

I close my journal shut, putting my hand firmly over the cover. "Nothing."

"Hmm." She wraps the end of one of her long, red-orange curls around the tips of her fingers over and over. "If I remember correctly from what we read in your diary, 'nothing' is just about right." She sighs and looks over her shoulder in the direction she came from. "I'm babysitting my cousins. They have story time here at three, so my aunt wanted me to bring them."

You're not doing a very good job of babysitting if your aunt is with you, and you're over here talking to me instead of watching them, I consider saying, but mainly I want her to leave.

She keeps twisting and twisting the end of her hair. "I saw you over here. Your shirt is so . . . splashy."

I look down at my T-shirt: an old tie-dye I found while searching for more creative outfit options again this morning. It's only pink with a little green dotted in, and it's probably too small, but the way Kendra says it makes it sound more like my shirt is made of spoiled mayonnaise.

"Anyway." She rolls her eyes like I'm the one who just said something stupid. "I saw you and said to myself, 'Oh wow. There's that Fiona girl from school. How funny. I haven't thought about her in ages. I should go say hi.' And—"

She makes a surprised face and reaches for her back pocket, taking out her phone.

"Would you look at that." She holds her screen out so I can see Cassie's picture splayed across it. "I just got a message from Cassie. Should I tell her you're here too? Maybe you'd like to say hi. Oh, wait. I forgot. She doesn't want to talk to you anymore because of the lame things you said about her and the rest of us, does she? Too bad."

Even if I wasn't already too shocked to speak, I'd still have no idea what to say back, but Kendra just laughs and walks back to the children's area, twisting and twisting that strand of her hair. I am utterly horrified, and sink lower in my chair, trying to hide my embarrassment.

That, and the renewed candle of anger that's become a flamethrower in my chest again.

"Fiona, you were in such a good mood this morning," Mom says as soon as I yank open the car door. "What happened?"

Without any warning, I start crying—hard.

Mom's as surprised as I am. "Oh now, now." She steers

the car away from the curb to a more private parking spot in the library lot. "What's all this?"

I cover my face with my hands as she leans over and folds me into her arms. There's so *much* that's all this, I don't know anymore where to start. One thing I do know is that what's wrong with my story is that the bad guys all die in the end and disappear. The truth is, Kendra will never go away, because Cassie will never stop being friends with her, which means Kendra will never forget me, or what happened. And so I never will, either.

"I hate everyone," I shout into my palms.

Mom smooths my hair. "Shhh, there. You hate who now?"

"Kendra Mack," I wail. "And Cassie. And just everyone."

Mom takes in a breath before saying anything. "Well, that doesn't sound very nice."

My shoulders shake. "*They* aren't nice!"

"Oh, honey," Mom says, turning toward me more. "I'm sorry about what you're going through. Are you sure this is how you want to deal with it, though?"

"I tried ignoring them," I say. "I tried being different, but—"

"You know that anyone who doesn't appreciate you for who you are—" she starts.

"You always say that," I yell over her. "You always jump

to telling me what to think and do, but it's just not that easy all the time. I can't always get away from people who don't like me. I can't pretend they aren't there."

Mom pulls back, looking at me different. "You're right," she says after a minute.

I wipe the itchy tears off my cheeks. "I am?"

She nods, gazing out the windshield, pointer fingernail flicking against the pad of her thumb a few times while she thinks.

"So, what do I do?" I ask when she still hasn't said anything.

"I don't know for sure," she admits. "But it might start with finding a solution that feels authentic to *you*, instead of turning into one of them."

Chapter Fifteen

After my outburst in the car, Mom still doesn't ask specifics about Kendra or Cassie, but instead we talk about anger, and revenge, and how not to let them control you. She tells me things I didn't know about the Divorce, and her difficulties with Dad, especially how quickly he introduced us to Jennifer. It surprises me but makes me feel better at once.

"We still had you two," she explains. "And I still wanted to raise you to be strong, beautiful women with healthy relationships with your parents, no matter what our problems with each other were. I knew bad-mouthing him wasn't going to help anything."

"So what did you do?"

"I did what you see me doing. I focus on the fact that he is your father, and that I want you to have a good relationship with him. I concentrate on the parts of his personality I appreciate, and stop fighting the ones I don't."

I'm still sniffling a little. "You make it sound so easy."

Mom laughs. "Oh no, it's not easy. It takes a lot of patience, and intention, and sometimes I fail. But if I consider you, and your sister, and the best version of myself, that helps. We tell ourselves stories in our head all the time about how we think things should be, how we want them to turn out, or what might be going on in someone else's head, but that isn't always best, or even the truth. For that we have to listen close."

"I think I need to do that with Evie," I say.

Mom's eyebrows go up. "Evie?"

"She didn't mean to get between me and Aja, and I know I should forgive her. We're talking again, but I still don't know how to say I'm sorry."

Mom strokes my hair some more. "Maybe there's a way of saying sorry without doing it the way you think you have to."

I briefly picture Cassie. "What if I stay mad forever? What if I can't apologize?"

Mom squeezes me in her strong arms. "Then you'll have to find a way to live with that too, I guess."

I don't want to live with any of these bad feelings, but before bed, I try to write about them a little—first thoughts, without criticism.

Your laugh will mock me through all the hallways
of my future, your betrayal one that repeats in my mind
like a frightening animated loop. What strength is there
in forgetting, only so you can backstab me over and over
again? Showing up when I least expect it, to rip the scabs
off all my healing wounds? What would I rather live
with? Letting this fear of continued hurt go, or letting you?
What can I accept? What could I, ever again?

It's mainly about Cassie, but when I read it over, I see it could be about pretty much anyone else. At least it helps to have that thought in my mind when Dad brings Leelu back to Mom's the next morning. To my surprise, the second she gets out of the car, Leelu comes running to wrap me in a giant hug. She's leaping and squeezing and trying to tell me six things at once, and though I don't like that Jennifer is so much a part of all these stories, the truth is I missed my sister, and I'm relieved to see she apparently missed me, too. When Dad grabs me up in a big hug, and says he's never going on vacation without me again, I know Mom's right that it's a lot easier to just be happy to have them back, even if it doesn't make me stop being mad at him for the rest.

When they leave, Mom takes Leelu and me to our favorite Japanese place for lunch, so we can celebrate and trade tales about what we've all done while we were apart. The sweet, excited way Leelu ask questions about writing camp, and my new friends, makes it a lot easier to concentrate on her favorite parts about Disneyland, instead of thinking about the rest.

Still, it makes me want to hit the reset button between us right away—to find something she and I can do together that will eclipse the whole Disneyland thing, good and bad.

And maybe repair things with Evie at the same time.

Leelu's back from Disney, I message her. **What are you doing tomorrow?**

It isn't an apology, but it feels like something right.

Salinas Farm! she types back right away. **Do you want to come?**

I'm surprised by the fast invitation, or that Mom says yes without a thought, but the next afternoon Leelu, Evie, her stepsister Kayda, and I are singing on the hayride around the farm, eating pie from the shop, playing in Evie and Kayda's treehouse afterward, and then watching them do gymnastics tricks on the swing set until it's time to come home. Just like Mom said, focusing on the parts of Evie I like helps replace the problematic business that happened between us with Aja. All that awkward stuff with Tyrick feels absolutely forever ago, anyway, and even if I hate how it happened, it did turn out a lot easier than telling him my real feelings.

Revision

There are things and then there are the things you can change them into once you've laid them out and examined them for what they could be. Perhaps not what you intended, but something they have become in the process of unspooling them. Put it down first, test it out later. The only way out is through. Nothing is static, everything is fluid. Changeable. Impermanent. Evie's skinnystrong limbs in a handspring flipping past the misunderstandings between us, making us friends again when I thought we weren't. Mom sturdy and strong on the surface, holding in confessions that encourage me to find my own bravery. Pencil becoming Tyrick. Old stories transforming into newer, better ones. Keeping the original heart at the core but helping it become something else. Telling my life in a different way. Letting it all go and grow with open hands and an honest, repairing heart.

"You have got to be kidding me," Sanders says when we're back in our writing pairs on Monday, sitting cross-legged together on the floor. Ellen's letting us write whatever kind of story we want the whole rest of this week, and I've decided at least Sanders needs to know the truth behind the Kandra/Callie story, so I can revise it into something that feels as good as getting back together with Evie this weekend did. Something I can accept.

I shake my head. "I am not."

He stares into space, picturing all of it, but then a slow, uneven smile appears. "That is *awful*. She really read your diary?"

His mischievous expression makes me laugh, even though there's still not anything funny about it.

"Out loud," I tell him. "On the bus."

"Who did?" Diamond says, craning her neck. She and Megan are stretched on their stomachs, not far from us. "Read your diary."

"A horrible girl at my school," I admit. "And my best friend sided with her."

Diamond's eyes go comically wide. Next to her, Megan covers most of her face with her hands and gasps, before Diamond's face shifts into cold seriousness.

"Girl who does something like that deserves to get lice," she says. "Or worse, bedbugs. Fleas. Roaches, something."

She makes a tsking sound. "Did she really do that to you?"

I laugh yes and thank her, because what she's said has given me an idea.

I turn to Sanders. "What if I wrote a story about a girl—a girl trying to be popular—who gets lice without knowing it, and then goes to a slumber party and gives it to all her popular friends?"

"And everybody has to get her head shaved!" he adds.

I'm doubtful. "Do they do that anymore?"

"Who cares? Whatever works for the story, right?"

I smile at him. "You're right. Whatever works."

Katie didn't want to be late to the party. It was her first time spending the night with Sandra Mackenzie, and Katie was already nervous. She didn't need tardiness to add to her anxieties, especially since she was still feeling guilty about not staying over with her best friend as they usually would. But Sandra was the most popular girl in school, and getting in with her and her gang of wealthy friends would elevate Katie's status far more than any of her old friends could.

The game she and her best friend had played at the wig shop had reminded Katie of their carefree old times together, but trying on a bunch of different silly hairstyles and taking on fake accents and attitudes to match them

*was for little girls. Katie was grown-up now. She didn't
need games like that anymore.*

*As she rang the doorbell and clutched her overnight bag
tighter to her chest, Katie reached up to scrunch her curly
black hair back into shape. When Sandra opened the door
and welcomed Katie with a big hug, neither of the girls
noticed the tiny black bug slipping from Katie's recently
tousled curls into Sandra's long yellow strands.*

Like Mom said about trying not to be angry, my story
takes a lot of effort. And at the end of the week, in spite
of several revisions, I'm still failing at it. I love the opening
scene—and the part in the barbershop where the popular
girls all get their heads shaved because Katie's given them
lice is funny—but after working on it so much, I'm starting to think the whole lice thing is a little too mean. Even
if Sanders likes it, once again I feel the ending is dumb.
Through all of camp, Ellen's stressed that good stories end
with some kind of change in the character. The way this
one wraps up, though, the main character is just bald and
ostracized by all her popular friends. I know she should
learn some kind of lesson, but I don't know what it is.

"It's because you don't start in the right place," Xi says
simply on our last day. She knew I was having trouble with

my draft, and offered to read it even though we're not offi-
cially partners.

"What do you mean?"

"I mean, getting lice isn't the problem." She hands my
printout back, decorated with her handwritten comments
in sparkly green pen.

I can't believe I might have to write something else all
over again.

"Of course it's the problem," I protest. "Look what happens when she does."

"But *why* does she get the lice? Acting out different
characters in the wig shop with her old friend is supercute,
but if the lice she gets from the wig are going to teach Katie
a lesson, there has to be a reason why she was doing it first,
right? Some prior behavior that causes the problem."

"When she goes to that slumber party, instead of to her
friend's house, like she usually would—"

"It's not her fault that the popular girls invited her over,
though," Xi says simply. "It's not even her fault that they
don't like her friend."

I stare at my paper, starting to feel a little uncomfortable.

"It's still really funny, though," Xi assures me. "I love
it when the girls are all crying at the barbershop together,

and the old friend happens to pass by and takes a picture of it. But see, that confused me too—what happens to the friend? The way you have it here, she doesn't really do anything except not get invited to the party, and then be at the right place at the right time to take the revenge picture. She doesn't even have a name. Maybe figuring out her role will help you with the rest of the story."

The idea of still not getting things right, even after so much work, is frustrating and disappointing. While Ellen says it's okay if the stories we share today still aren't final— that writing evolves over time, and sometimes that means not working on something for days, or even months—I'm not interested in this taking a long time. We're halfway through the summer already, and there are still too many loose ends. I hoped at least I could write one complete story.

But Xi's input has given me a creepy feeling on the back of my neck for another reason. If, in my story, Katie is really Cassie, and her old friend is really me—then I'm not sure what my role in everything is, either.

Chapter Sixteen

O nce creative writing camp is over (and my friends and I have all swapped contact information), I'm ready to give my brain a break. Leelu and I still have some work to do putting Disneyland behind us too, so first thing at home Friday afternoon, I page through my old English notebook for that unfinished list of things we wanted to do this summer. The one she forgot about when Jennifer showed up with end-of-school presents.

She's happy when I show it to her, though, and we spend the rest of the evening adding more to it. When we share our ideas with Mom and Maritza, they're both energized, and since we're back on our regular parent rotation (which means another whole week of not having to see Jennifer), with their help we manage to do a pretty good job on our list.

Sister Summer: A List by Fiona and Leelu Coppleton
   Go to the country club pool every day (Except if it ever rains!)
   Volunteer at the homeless shelter
   Force Mom to get some fresh air and take us on a hike
   See a double feature
   Attend a race at the Mazda Raceway
   Spend one whole day doing nothing but playing Barbies (Fiona note: even if 12 is too old)
   Read at least one book a week
   Roller-skate
   Wash Mom, Dad, & Maritza's cars for allowance
   Build a fort entirely of Legos
   Learn about something new (Still need ideas)

Daylong fun at Teamer Park
Trying every flavor of saltwater taffy at Cannery Row

Those last two are Dad's idea, which he inserts as soon as Leelu tells him about the list when we get to his house on Monday.

"Jennifer read about Teamer on that Family Finds blog,"

he says, taking my notepad to add it. "And we haven't been to Cannery Row in a long time. How come going on the boat's not on here, either?"

Leelu hops up and down. Dad's boat is one of her favorite activities no matter what time of year, but Jennifer happens to love it too. It's why I never included it on the list (and, also, because I got sick the last two times we went, though no one else seems to remember). I hoped Leelu wouldn't bring it up, either. But of course Dad wants to do things right away that involve Jennifer, and of course Leelu is excited about his suggestions.

It's the opposite of the point.

"You hate Cannery Row," I say to Leelu, since I already know it's useless trying to talk her out of the boat.

"No, I don't." She scowls.

"When Maritza took us, all you did was whine about how crowded and boring it was."

"Nuh-uh. I went there with Harlow for her birthday. We did a scavenger hunt and it was so awesome. Dad, can we go to the Ghirardelli place first?"

"Why don't we go to the park Friday, and leave Cannery Row up for debate?"

"Don't you have to work?" I ask him. Friday we're supposed to go to the aquarium and on a picnic with Maritza, and then spend the afternoon at the pool, so that we can keep up our record of attending every day. I don't want to forfeit that even for a place as majestic as Teamer Park with all its rocks-and-ocean beauty, but I especially don't want to if it means spending a whole day with the Princess Twosome.

"Most of my clients are on summer vacation too." Dad sounds a little hurt. "I think one day with my daughters can be spared. I know Jennifer has personal leave she needs to use up."

"But what about Maritza? This is her job, you know. She counts on us. And she was just on vacation."

He laughs a little. "That's a good point. Why don't you two call some friends and we'll take a whole group. That way I'll need both their help."

Leelu's screech of excitement practically shakes the kitchen cabinets. "Can I bring Jessica? And Harlow? And maybe Reed?"

"Fiona, what about you?" Dad turns to the cutting board to start chopping vegetables for our stir fry.

It occurs to me that if Leelu has her real friends with her, at least she'll be distracted from her shiny new bejeweled one who also happens to be Dad's girlfriend. And if I invite Evie, Leelu will hopefully have more fun with us than with Jennifer.

In fact, I think, the more people to distract Leelu with the better, which gives me an idea that might help not just me, but Evie too.

Though I'm uncertain how well Evie and Sanders are going to get along, they're my two closest friends now, and I want them to know each other. They'll keep me from having to talk to Jennifer, too, but I admittedly have a secret third agenda. My hunch is that Aja's given Evie (and Evie's parents) the wrong idea about what relationships with boys and girls are like. If Evie sees how funny and cool Sanders is, she might feel less intimidated because boys are around, and her parents might relax, too.

But it's not as easy as I want it to be.

When Sanders arrives at Dad's house, he stretches out a hand to shake with Evie, saying, "Nice to meet you," but Evie blushes and her "Hi" is barely audible.

"Sanders is my friend from creative writing camp," I try. "He writes really funny stories. And he helped me a lot with mine."

"Fiona's an awesome writer," he says.

"Tell her what kind of stories you do, though." I nudge him.

"Oh, you know, mostly political commentaries involving

giant bears and gerbils, and the end of the human race."

Evie scrunches her nose, not sure whether he's kidding or not. I'm not really sure, either.

Unlike Aja, though (when she's around River anyway), Sanders clues in immediately that he hasn't landed on a common topic. As we drive to the park he asks Evie about her summer instead. He seems genuinely interested in what she might have to say, but to my disappointment she only gives him one-word answers, like "Camp," and "Yeah," and "Fine."

By the time we get to Teamer, I feel it was a giant mistake to make Evie and Sanders friends; Evie's just too uncomfortable, and Sanders is too determined to give up trying. My attempts at being sweet to Evie and jokey with Sanders at the same time are stressful, and make me wish for a brief second that I could just enjoy the day with a best friend I don't have to work so hard at being with—like the one I used to have before she decided she was better than me.

But that's not the way it is. This is. And if it's going to work I'll have to make it.

"We're swimming first, right?" Sanders says when we get to Teamer.

Evie looks at me hopefully. So there's something we can agree on. Around us Leelu and her friends start chanting some swimming song from a cartoon they all know, so we spread out our towels, apply sunscreen, and help Maritza set up the umbrella.

To my happiness and relief, Jennifer makes a fuss about getting her hair wet, and won't go in the water. As soon as everyone's ready, Sanders runs as hard as he can through the sand, plunging into the giant rolling waves, and the rest of us follow, leaving Jennifer behind with Maritza, who doesn't like to swim in the ocean, either. Dad dives straight under, while Leelu and her two friends shriek as the cold water smacks their skin. Evie wants to step in a little more carefully, so I stay with her, but when we reach the others out in the calmer water, I concentrate on nothing else except not getting water up my nose, and having fun. We swim and splash around, try to hold ourselves in handstands against the current, and then practice dolphin dives and humpback whale leaps. Dad lets Leelu climb up onto his shoulders and jump off, and soon he's become a human diving board for her and both her friends. It makes me think of doing chicken fights next—me, Evie, and Sanders, with the littler kids on our backs.

"Throw us together, Daddy!" Leelu cries, crawling through the surf to Dad for another round. When she reaches him, she stretches out her hand to me. I'm probably too big to be thrown, but Dad's strong, and that is one of our favorite things. I start bobbing my way over, and he raises an arm in greeting, but I realize it isn't to me.

"You all look like you're having too much fun," Jennifer calls behind us.

"Jenny!"

Leelu lets go of Dad and dog-paddles to where Jennifer's carefully stepping out to us, arching her neck to keep her hair dry even when waves only splash her stomach.

"Come on," I say to Evie and Sanders. "Let's get some sun."

Sanders doesn't hesitate. "Body surf," he commands, and to my delight, even Evie stretches out her hands and ducks her face into the next wave. We splay out on the beach so that the water rushes up around our legs and feet. I'm not really ready to be done swimming, but at least I'm away from Jennifer.

Sanders tosses a shell into the water and looks toward Teamer Cliff. "Have you ever done that?"

"No way." Evie's shaking her head.

The cliff is a giant outcrop of rock that juts out at what looks like an impossible angle over the ocean: wider at the very top than at the bottom. There's a steep trail up to it, and near the pinnacle you have to climb over some big boulders, but when you get there, from what I've seen in the pictures anyway, the stone makes a perfectly smooth jumping-off platform. Usually when cliffs and the ocean meet like that, the rocks at the base and the powerful tide combine to make it far too dangerous to jump off, but because of the way this one is formed, and the curved inlet it hangs over, it creates nature's perfect high-dive.

But it's still super high and scary-looking.

"We should do it," Sanders asserts.

Evie looks out at the water. "I'll stay here I think."

"You can't be scared, are you?" Sanders seems genuinely astonished.

Beyond them I see Jennifer already wading back to the beach, playfully dragging Leelu, who's gripping her waist, in what looks like our made-up game, Rescue Mermaid.

When Evie says nothing, Sanders shakes his head, wet curls sticking against his face. "Do you know how special that formation is? Not to mention the biggest thrill of your life? It would be a crime if I didn't make you go up. I promise you it's safe. They wouldn't advertise everywhere about it if it wasn't. They'd get sued."

Evie bites her lip and looks so scared she might cry. Beyond her, Jennifer collapses on the sand. Leelu kneels over her, saying something I don't need to fully hear to know she wants to make sand sculptures next.

I could probably do the jump if Sanders coached me, but I can't just leave Evie behind.

"What if we go watch?" I ask her. "And judge the way he jumps, like the Olympics?" Evie is obsessed with the Olympics. Gymnastics is her favorite, but she really likes all of it. Even the weight lifting.

"That's exactly it," Sanders agrees.

Evie looks up at him from under her eyelashes. "Same scoring system?"

"Whatever you say."

"Come on." I stand up.

"But what's the criteria?" Evie wants to know.

I let Sanders answer her, and go up to the umbrella to tell Maritza where we're going. She immediately insists on coming, too.

"Sissie, over here!" Leelu calls, finally seeing me.

"We're doing Teamer Cliff," I tell her.

"Me, too." Sand clings to her brown knees as she stands up.

"No, you can't," I say, firm. "Stay here with your friends."

I turn my back on my sister to cross the stretch of beach between here and the cliff. It's only about fifty yards, but the whole way Maritza anxiously reminds us what to do if we get caught in an undertow. I don't want her concern to freak Evie out all over again, but she seems too caught up in talking to Sanders about his dive plan to notice.

"He's actually nice," she tells me, once we're positioned

on the rocks, closely but safely enough to see Sanders when he comes down. Maritza's a little farther off in a shady spot, but where she can still see all three of us.

"He was my favorite person in camp," I answer.

She looks at me, doubtful. "Usually boys are so loud or so gross. I don't understand why Aja always wants to hang out with them."

"You don't like River?"

She shrugs. "He's okay, I guess. It's her I don't like when River's around."

I nod, understanding completely.

"I'm sorry about what happened with all that, by the way," she says, quiet. "I mean, you know, Tyrick."

I'm unsure how to respond, since I don't want this to turn into an Aja-bashing conversation. For one, Evie's her best friend, but also, suddenly talking about Aja again makes me miss her.

"She still won't talk to me," I concede, shielding my eyes from the sun to search for Sanders in the trail of people moving up the side of the steep formation.

"But you said you didn't want to hear from her. She thinks she's giving you space!"

I guess I did say something like that in the last text I sent.

"Are you and Sanders gonna start going out?" Evie asks before I say anything.

"What?"

"That's why you wanted us both to come today, right? So you could see him but it wouldn't seem like a date? It's okay if it is. Just promise you won't stop hanging out with me one-on-one, okay? I hate that."

I'm sad she thinks she has to ask, though it does explain some things. If Aja, like me, truly needs friends around to be allowed on anything that could be considered a possible "date," it makes sense why she got mad that I didn't want to see Tyrick anymore. I'm not sure I'd have acted how she did about it, but I suppose if I were Aja I would've gotten upset, too.

But it's still silly for Evie to think I want to go out with Sanders.

"Evie, having a boy as a friend isn't the same thing as having a crush."

She scrunches her nose again. "But they're so obnoxious. All they care about is blood, boogers, and comic books. And they want to do things like that." She gestures to Teamer Cliff. I look again too, and spot Sanders waving at us from the top, only three people away from his turn.

I wave back to him and he smiles wide. Evie's right—boys can be obnoxious. River certainly was with all that revolting talk at the mall. But Aja herself proved that afternoon that girls can be just as gross. Plenty of boys like things other than violence and snot, anyway. And I know from personal experience that they can be just as nice and helpful as girls, whether you're writing about sword-wielding ninjas or not.

"I guess it isn't as simple as us versus them," I tell her. "Not if you're open to it, anyway."

"You're so smart."

She's not looking at me, but watching as Sanders approaches the edge, bends his knees, and takes his jump. It's a perfectly fine, average-person leap, but halfway down, he somehow turns his body around and enters the water in a straight-arrow perfect dive.

"Let's do it," Evie says, strong.

"What?"

She nods toward Sanders. "Let's jump."

"Are you serious?"

She stands up, wiping rock dust off her bottom and looking determined. "It's not really that high. And Sanders is right about it being safe. We're going to be in eighth grade next year, and then high school. Maybe it's time for me to stop being such a chicken about everything all the time."

"Evie, are you for real?"

"Maybe not," she laughs. "But hurry up before I freak out and change my mind."

I obey, and we head across the pebbly part of the inlet's beach. When Sanders gets out of the water to join us he raises his arms over his head in victory. We climb the rocky trail together, Sanders pointing out the best places to step. The path is steeper and rockier than I expect, and I consider going back for my shoes, but Evie keeps pushing steadily ahead of me, so if she's not turning back, I can't, either. Near the top—the part that always looks scariest to me—Sanders shows us places to put our feet and hands, almost like a natural ladder.

It's nowhere as bad as I thought.

"Wow," Evie says when we finish climbing up.

"Told you," Sanders says.

"How do we go?" Evie asks him, watching the people ahead of us jump off.

"It's not as scary as it looks," he assures us, "but you can't think about it too hard. You have to just do it to find out."

"Like freewriting," I say, moving into line with Evie. She's staring ahead at the edge like she's an action hero making a life-or-death decision, but I know she's going through with it.

"Just do it to find out," Evie repeats when it's our turn, and without any more thoughts or words, we step to the edge, and jump.

Leaping: for Evie

"It's not as scary as it looks," he said. "But you can't think about it too hard. You have to just do it to find out."

Leaping flying trying new things, jumping away from all my worry and sadness, plunging into the scary blue of the abyss that turns out to be only a cool embrace to enfold me and lift me back, back to the surface where we can look up and see how far we fell, tracing the air with our eyes the distance we've come, that long terrible fall that wasn't so terrible. As you look up in wonder at it and yourself, perhaps you spot the girl you were before the jump, the one you left at the top. The one you discarded to become someone else, or just you, different, here in the water, trying new things and making new friends, unable to imagine or remember what it was like to be afraid. Even the thrill in your stomach as you dropped is gone, transformed by the fall and the water and the smiles of your friends into something so happy it dissipates into the bubbles around you. It doesn't have to be us versus them, I said, and she jumped, and took me with her, and now she's changed and I'm changed but we're still together, the same friends but both of us somehow different.

The next morning Dad's at the kitchen table, but not in his racquetball clothes.

"Aren't you playing?" I ask.

He stands, moving stiffly after our park adventure yesterday. "The Fosters will be here soon to pick your sister up for her playdate with Reed. I thought afterward you and I might spend some time, just the two of us. So think about what you might want to do."

He leaves the kitchen and I watch after him, surprised, but immediately full of dread. I wasn't rude yesterday, but I'm sure he noticed how much I was avoiding Jennifer. Probably he wants to get me alone to lecture me about how I need to be nicer to her. There's only one thing I can think of that will throw Dad off enough to keep us from having that conversation, and that's shopping. I've wanted more interesting outfits anyway, and after talking about Aja with Evie I remember the perfect place. I rush back for my phone, looking for the Plato's Closet bookmark I made when Aja mentioned it when we went to the mall at the beginning of the summer. Though taking Dad on my first thrift store trip might be crazy, at least it will give us something else to focus on instead of how much I dislike his girlfriend.

Without argument or protest, when I suggest the outing, Dad says it sounds fun. And instead of lecturing me in the car, he wants to play our old music game, where he chooses a song by someone classic like Bill Withers or Otis Redding on the stereo, and sees if I can guess who it is in the first twenty seconds.

We don't get a lot of rounds in, because Plato's Closet isn't far away, but it is definitely in a different neighborhood than ours—one with coffeehouses, food trucks, tattoo shops, and lots of cool-looking high schoolers milling around in the sunshine. There's a giant mural of horses transforming into birds along one whole wall of a building, and across the street there's a line of shops selling vintage furniture and clothes. I'm exhilarated and intimidated both at the same time.

"Like law school days," Dad says, looking around. "This the right place?"

I can only nod. The combination of this cool neighborhood and Dad's playfulness is throwing me off. Dad holds the shop door open for me, smiling excitedly. I want to smile back too, but as soon as my eyes adjust to the dark interior after being in the bright sunshine outside, the first thing I see is Cheyenne Taylor—Kendra Mack's second-best friend— standing at the rear of the store. She has her back to us, studying a rack of shoes, but I recognize her by her long, wavy blond hair and her matching giraffe legs. Those, and the odd-looking denim bag that apparently

Kendra made Cheyenne stop wearing the first time she brought it to school. I have no idea what someone like Cheyenne is doing in a place like this, but I definitely don't want her seeing me. There's no way I can give her even the slightest opportunity to make any snide comments about diaries, or Cassie, especially not in front of Dad.

"Fee, I think you'll be more interested in what's this way," Dad offers, when I try to duck behind the nearest rack. Which turns out to be men's jackets.

I follow reluctantly, trying to keep as many wildly dressed mannequins between me and Cheyenne as possible. Though Cheyenne is the opposite of Izzy—the nicest one of Kendra's friends instead of the meanest—I'm sure she'd blab that I was here with my father to Kendra. And to Cassie.

Dad's oblivious. "So what is it you're looking for?" he asks, flipping through a bunch of tank tops, like he'd have any idea what to get me. Before the Divorce, Dad always left the clothes shopping to Mom, unless we needed something for a special occasion. Since then he's taken Leelu and me to get a few basics—jeans, say, or new shoes—but we've never done this kind of shopping before. The kind where you're just looking and waiting for something fantastic to jump out. Now with Cheyenne here, it feels like the most horrible and embarrassing day to try it for the first time. I'm tempted to tell Dad this wasn't what I was expecting and we should just leave, but if I do he'll ask me why—probably too loud—which would only bring more attention over here.

I shrug, keeping an eye on Cheyenne, who has moved over to the sunglasses. "I don't really know."

"Dresses? Tops? Maybe something like this?" Dad holds up a pair of orange pleather leggings.

Of course he's going to be mortifying.

"Okay, okay," he says, seeing my face. "Serious. I get it."

To keep some distance between us, I move to a separate rack of shirts. If Cheyenne does see me, she at least won't see me with my *dad*. He doesn't seem to mind at all, and starts searching in earnest. I find it hard to do the same thing very well while keeping an eye on Cheyenne, though. After several fumbling moments, where I'm mostly accidentally pulling things off their hangers, Dad comes over holding seven or eight different tops. They're all in my size, and—even more surprising—are the kind that will fit into the artier, non-Cassie wardrobe I'm dreaming of.

"Wow, Dad."

"This one I thought would go with that new beret of yours."

I hold up the black tank top. The metallic sheen of the

fabric feels a little too punk rock for me, but I'm so caught off guard that he noticed and remembered my new hat, I take the whole pile from him.

"Well, go see if I'm right."

I crane my neck to give the entire store a careful, sneaky look. Cheyenne must have left when I was examining Dad's choices, because she's nowhere. So I relax a little, and even let Dad follow me to the dressing rooms. As soon as I pull on the metallic tank top in my curtained stall, it's clear it *is* too punk (and a little too big), but I decide to show Dad anyway since he was so excited. Plus, it might give him a better idea of what to pick next round.

Right as I pull back the curtain, there's Cheyenne, walking past.

"Oh." She stops so that we don't ram into each other. When she realizes who I am she tucks her thick blond hair behind both ears, looking surprised, and guilty. "Fiona. Do you shop here?"

My whole body is going through that fight-or-flight thing we learned about in biology, but in between flashes of panic, I picture me and Evie yesterday, jumping even though we were scared. And it not being that bad.

"This is my first visit," I somehow tell her, calm as possible.

Her face lights up and she touches my arm in confidence.

"There's so much great stuff, right? My sister used to work here. She'd bring home the coolest outfits, because a lot of times people just leave bags of what the shop rejects in the parking lot. Too lazy to go donate it somewhere else I guess, but that meant she brought whatever she wanted home for free."

I nod, like I get it, but mostly I can't believe Cheyenne is being so nice to me. Or is admitting that her sister wears, essentially, other people's trash.

"She's home from college now," she goes on. "We like to come here for nostalgia. Anyway, that top is cute. But it's probably a little big. No offense."

I look down, still not having any idea what to think or say. "Thanks."

"The best days to shop here are—oh. Hang on." Her phone is blaring an old Iggy Azalea song from the depths of her denim bag. "Hi, Kendra Mack," she says, bright, without even checking the screen. I remember their stupid "unspoken" rule about calling each other by first and last names. "What's up?"

For privacy, Cheyenne lets the heavy curtain of her hair fall back in front of her face, and ducks into the closest empty stall. Not knowing what else to do, I go out to show Dad the top—he agrees with Cheyenne that it's too big—but when I come back she's still talking.

"Ugh, I know," I overhear. "So gross. But when Sienna's home she gets to do whatever she wants, and you know Janice still won't let me stay at home alone. So that means I had to get dragged here."

I change back into my own shirt as quickly as possible, and take my stack of untried-on tops back out into the store. I tell Dad I decided I want to find skirts or bottoms to go with them before trying the rest on, which he doesn't seem to mind. We're still at it when I see Cheyenne finally slide out of the dressing room, looking disappointed. Confused by this crazy contrast in one of Kendra's friends, I can't help watching her with some of Cassie's and my old *Harriet the Spy* action as she goes over to another tall, blond girl flipping through dresses. Cheyenne says something to her sister, who makes a face and starts to protest, until Cheyenne says something else, something about "I'll pay you back"—and they both leave, neither of them looking very happy.

"Friend from school?" Dad asks, noticing me staring.

"No," I say, trying to focus again on the skirts in front of me. But to be honest, after what just happened in the dressing room, I don't know what to call Cheyenne anymore at all.

Chapter Seventeen

Monday night at Mom's, another weird thing happens. Leelu's gotten out our list, and is asking Mom for her opinions on what last things are most important as summer ends.

"Oh, that reminds me," Mom says, reaching for a pencil. "I thought about Hearst Castle."

"Really!?" Leelu and I say at the same time.

"Serena mentioned it the other day. Sounds like Tess has got the travel bug in her again, now that she and Howie are really married. They're taking Cassie and Lana on a road trip for their belated honeymoon. I think Hearst Castle is one of the stops."

"Like Sleeping Beauty!" Leelu cries.

I fix an interested half smile on my face while Leelu speculates with Mom about how great it would be to live in a castle, so long as there weren't as many thorns, but really I'm fighting the weirdest feeling. Cassie is off somewhere with her newly married grandparents, and I didn't know the first thing about it. We haven't even talked about her new cousin, but apparently now they're all on a vacation I'm totally ignorant about. She could be anywhere in the state, and I had no idea.

I tell Mom and Leelu I'll be back in time to help with dinner, and head to my room.

You were half gone from my mind—a dandelion with only a scrap of fuzz left, needing only one more final breath to scatter the rest of you to the wind—but I look now across the grass of my feelings and there you are, popped up all over the place, a dozen different puffy heads and more there and there and there: weeds of you that require the most powerful poisons to kill. Even though I've found new flowers better than simply weeds with which to fill my garden, suddenly the air is full of you again, and you stick to my hair and my clothes, unshakable.

Why even after all this work is there still a hole in me the shape of you?

Why do I still have all these questions when you've obviously found your answers?

Why do I still wish you had been there not just to see me leap, but to take my hand in your hand and jump with me?

Can I ever imagine a future when we could, without letting go of the rest?

Just as I finish writing that sentence, a message comes in: **Please you have to go shopping with me.** It's Sanders.

??? I type back.

My dads always make me go back-to-school shopping, he explains. **It's unbearable. If I tell them I'm taking you instead at least I know I'll end up with something cool.**

I smile. **Where and when?**

Three days later (after insisting to Dad that Sanders is just a friend, plus letting him cross-reference this with Mom, and both of Sanders's dads), Sanders's dad Paulo is taking the two of us to Del Monte.

"Okay, sweetie, you sure this is all right?" Paulo asks, dropping us off.

"Yes, Dad." Sanders groans.

"And Fiona, you promise you will not let him walk out of here with a bunch of tacky garbage?"

I tell Sanders's dad I'm not interested in making my

friend look like an idiot on the first day of school.

"Sanders will come out with plenty of respectable outfits."

Paulo smiles, white teeth against tan skin. "You are a good friend to him."

I grin back, shut the car door, and wave good-bye.

"Okay, so," Sanders says, once we're both free among the shops and corridors. "Where do we start?"

Usually I'm the one getting advice on my wardrobe, not giving it, so I'm unsure where to begin. Until I remember Aja and her accessories.

"Maybe shoes? Or a belt or a hat? Then we can build around it."

"As long as it's something other than blue and gray." He tugs at the T-shirt he's wearing. "The dads believe in a lot of mix-and-match pieces."

I don't know the significance of blue and gray, but I more than get that he wants something different. And after five separate shops with Sanders, I also get why his fathers have made him stick to two colors. Sanders is pickier about his clothes than Leelu is about her movies, and nearly everything I select is met with an "I don't think so" or a disapproving look. After an hour, we've been to every clothing store that will have his size, with only one red T-shirt to show for it.

I point out that his dad will be back in an hour, trying not to sound too exasperated.

"How about we get some food?" Sanders suggests. "That way I can focus."

I'm hungry too, not to mention tired from all the rejection, so we go for hoagies, chips, and giant sodas at a nearby vendor. As we take our table in the central pavilion, Sanders tells me about a new shogun movie his cousin showed him. It's hard to concentrate on what he's saying, though, because a distracting, familiar voice is cutting through the air behind us.

When I finally realize who it is, the back of my neck prickles, and my whole torso tenses up.

Sanders notices the shift in my mood. "What is it?"

"Shh." I cock my ear so I can listen better. Through the surrounding din, I clearly hear Izzy's stony voice: "Say he made her the main character in a video game he's designing."

"That's stupid"—Kendra. "We don't know if he can actually program them, just because he's president of the Losers for Virtual Reality Club."

"Who else is in that?" Cheyenne asks, sounding genuinely interested. I wonder if she has that denim purse with her this time.

"You're so dumb," Izzy says.

"You guys—just look at this."

I sneak a glance over my shoulder, taking in Kendra's back as she leans over the table to offer her phone to Izzy and Cheyenne, who are in the seats across from her. Neftali is there too, but she's next to Kendra so has her back to me.

"Is she *seven?*" Neftali laughs. It's the exact tone I've heard Cassie try to copy more than once.

"Make Cory tell her he wants a selfie," Izzy suggests. "But a gross one. Something really embarrassing. Cassie's so pathetic she'll do it."

Turning back to Sanders, I feel like I'm falling off Teamer Cliff again, hitting the water with a splash. But instead of sinking into the gentle, supporting ocean, I'm falling into cold, hard reality. Apparently, they're pretending to be Cassie's most secret crush: the one they know about only because they read my diary. I never used Cory's real name in any of my entries—I know because I checked, several times—but she must've eventually told them herself. It stings to know she's gotten close enough to share something like that with them, but what stands out more is that obviously they don't think it's cool.

Instead they're using it to make fun of her.

"Fiona, are you all right?" Sanders asks.

I hold up a finger and aim my ear again at the girls behind us.

"Priceless," Kendra says after a moment of waiting.

"What are you going to do with it?" Neftali jeers.

"Whatever I want."

Kendra's voice has the same mocking tone it did that day in the library—the one I'm sure she used when she was reading my diary out loud on the bus. Something about it makes me picture the ninjas from my writing camp story. Or Kendra's thick red curls crawling with tiny bugs.

"What are you doing?" Sanders harsh-whispers when I pick up my soda and push my chair back.

"Just saying hi to some friends."

Once I stand, I can see that Kendra's group isn't even three tables away from us. No wonder they felt so loud. But it also means I don't have time to second-guess what I'm doing. I cross the distance between our tables in only a few strides, clenching my soda cup in my hand so hard I worry my fingers might punch through the Styrofoam. The other girls sense someone moving toward them and all look up, but I'm not intimidated this time. I lift the cup to shoulder height, and then turn the entire thirty-two ounces of my giant soda over Kendra's head.

"What??" she shrieks, leaping up. Her glossy coils are stuck to her face and neck with Sprite, and her phone is swimming in a big puddle that's threatening to drip into Izzy's lap.

Which makes Izzy stand too, though slower than Kendra. Like a snake uncoiling. "Oh, you are *finished*, Diary Downer."

Thoughts of immediately transferring to a new school are flashing through my head, but I'm too full of anger, and adrenaline, to back down. Kendra's trying to mop soda out of her hair with paper napkins; Neftali leans across to help, getting her designer T-shirt soaked in the process. Cheyenne is looking at me with the same confusion I felt when I saw her at Plato's Closet, and Izzy's scowl has become far less threatening, since now I'm pretty sure it's the only thing she knows how to do. These girls violated my privacy, humiliated me in front of nearly the whole seventh grade, and on top of that stole my best friend. But somehow, with the help of other friends, I've turned my shattered life into something good, and managed to make myself stronger.

I meet Izzy's eye. "You'd better watch out," I warn her. "Because I'm not afraid of you anymore."

"Yeah, I bet." Though she sounds less than convinced.

I keep my eyes locked on hers until she's the one who finally breaks our stare. Only then do I turn my back on them and return to Sanders.

"Whoa" is all he says, still watching behind me.

I look too. Neftali and Cheyenne are trying to clean up

the mess, but more Sprite spills onto Kendra's sandals, and she yelps.

"That's Kandra Black, isn't it?" Sanders murmurs.

Eyes still on them, I nod.

"And you just totally vanquished her."

Kendra's friends give up on the sticky table and huddle around her to shuffle in a group to the bathrooms. A few kids are taking photos. Kendra's pretending everything's completely fine, but even Izzy looks ruffled. It feels wonderful. And satisfying. And really, really funny, especially when I turn again to Sanders and see the reason he hasn't said anything else is that he's laughing too hard.

"That," he gasps, trying to sit up straight, "was way better than lice."

I bust up laughing too. "Thanks."

We settle back into eating. Between bites, Sanders reenacts the whole thing for me, including Kendra's shocked and horrified squeal of rage when I dumped the soda on her. It's funny the way he does it, and I'm glad he was there, but as I listen, I can tell the smile on my face doesn't quite penetrate my heart. Yes, I stood up to Kendra. Once I realized what she was doing, something clicked inside of me. Nobody deserves friends as mean as those girls—not even Cassie. But now Cassie's miles and miles away, off with her cousin, and she'll never hear about what happened. Kendra certainly won't tell her, and from the look on her face, not even Izzy will breathe a word. Probably it won't keep them from being mean to her, either. So even if I was sticking up for my old friend, it won't make a difference. Even though Sanders keeps spontaneously chuckling about it as we move from store to store—there's something terribly lonely inside me, knowing I'll never get to tell Cassie about it myself.

Chapter Eighteen

Apparently dumping soda on your worst enemy is a great way to inspire your friend into some serious shopping, because after lunch, Sanders whirls through a single store and comes out with a whole new wardrobe. After all the try-ons, plus the crazy lingering high of the soda dumping, when Paulo drops me back off at Dad's (because Mom is on her way to San Francisco for a business trip) I'm exhausted. The last thing I want to see is Jennifer's white Lexus in our driveway. I open the front door, slow, hoping she and Leelu won't hear me.

But right away Jennifer calls, "Hi, Fee," from the kitchen, followed by Leelu's cheerful hello. I've tried demonstrating to Jennifer in the past (by not responding) how much I dislike her calling me that, but apparently it hasn't worked. I should ignore her again and head straight to my room, but I'm too curious to see what new bonding experience she and Leelu are having. I step silently across the living room and carefully peer around the edge of the pass-through between our high-ceilinged dining room and the kitchen.

I'm not sneaky enough, though, because they both immediately look up.

"Why are you here?" I demand when I'm caught.

Jennifer's big smile drops a little. She tries to hide it by licking a finger that's sticky with cookie dough. "Your sister's helping me make cookies. It's my terrible secret—that I can't really cook."

"But what happened to Maritza?"

"Jenny's the babysitter now!" Leelu bounces on her stool.

"Well, not quite." Jennifer hands the spoon to Leelu and tells her to finish up the last row on their cookie sheet. To me, she more carefully says, "Your father and I planned a special dinner with you girls tonight, so my boss let me take off for the weekend early. I thought I'd spend some extra time with you two beforehand. Maritza's fine. She'll be here tomorrow with you just like normal."

I'm not liking this answer. Not one bit. Maritza's never been released early before, not unless Mom or Dad get time off.

"Where are we going?"

Jennifer's lips smile, but her eyes flicker with doubt. "It's a surprise. Your dad should be home by six. I'd love it if you'd make cookies with us until then." She pats one of Leelu's newly unbraided pigtail pom-poms, and my stomach curls as my sister flashes her a loving grin.

Of course I'd love to make cookies with Leelu, especially after pouring a giant cup of soda on the most powerful girl in my entire grade, but I certainly don't want to do that with *her* around.

Dad comes in the front door then, booming, "I'm home early too, so it's time to get changed! Fancy dinner clothes for you all."

"Where are we going?" I insist again, over Jennifer and Leelu's happy sounds.

Dad lifts an arm over his head like a dramatic waiter. "Passionfish!"

Passionfish is even better than Sardine Factory. But I'm not giving in.

"Jennifer can't go like that," I say, indicating her cargo capris.

She and Dad exchange a look.

"I brought something," she says. "I'll get changed in the guest room."

"Sissie, we can get oysters and do I spy with the boats," Leelu interrupts.

I'm too mad to get excited. This is not what I want at all, even if my afternoon hadn't been such a roller coaster. "I'm tired of going out all the time," I tell Dad. "I don't know why we can't just stay home for once, on our own."

I stress *our own* as firmly as I can and then stomp off to my room. I know I don't have a choice, since they've obviously both orchestrated this "surprise," but maybe I'll spite Dad and refuse to order anything, even at the best seafood restaurant in possibly the whole world.

No one cares that I'm giving them all the silent treatment in the car. The second we sit down, Dad orders champagne, and then ginger ale for me and Leelu, which she and Jennifer have apparently dubbed "beauty juice" while at Disneyland. It transforms my resentment about this evening into real dread. If I had my journal, I'd let loose and fill pages with creative insults and complaints, but right now all I can think is *No*.

"We have something to tell you," Dad says when our glasses are filled. He takes Jennifer's hand. "After such a great day all together at the park, we know that's what we want for always. It's a little sooner than we expected"— he smiles at Jennifer, who's smiling back at him big and warm—"but we've decided to get married, so that we can all be a family. We wanted to tell you together, since that's how we'll be from now on."

Leelu claps and holds up her ginger ale in a grown-up, toast-like way, but my blood turns to ice as Jennifer clinks glasses with Leelu, and Dad looks at them both proudly. Jennifer says something about how much we mean to her, blinking back misty tears. She knows she'll never be our mom, she goes on, but she hopes she can be a confidante and a comfort to us in her own way. Leelu immediately starts asking about the wedding, and if we get to be flower girls, or carry the ring, but I can barely listen. Instead I picture myself throwing a fit, which is probably why Dad brought us to such a fancy public place to tell us. Jennifer is still blubbering something about never imagining she'd have such beautiful kids, and the dreamy smile on Leelu's face is all I need to think ahead to when Jennifer's living with us (Dad says not before the end of the year, but it is happening eventually), and I'll have to share my sister forever.

I stand up and excuse myself to the bathroom. I'm too angry to cry, and too sad to make a scene. It's not just because of Dad and Jennifer's announcement, but because there's no one around who can fully understand the severity of this situation. Sanders would start another revenge plot, Evie would just try to make me feel better by telling me about her own parents' divorce, and Mom might not even know yet.

There's only one person who could make this better, but she's the one I'm still supposed to hate the most.

Lost, forever lost. Gone, forever gone. Alone, forever alone. Empty, forever empty, is all I can write when we finally get home.

Wanted to let you sleep since it seemed you needed it, my phone blings from Dad in the morning. **I'm taking a break from work so we can have lunch at 1:00. Hope you three have fun together until then.**

It's a stiff message to receive the moment I wake up, but since I barely spoke to Dad the rest of the night, I'm not surprised. I didn't set an alarm because I wanted to sleep through his leaving the house, and luckily, he didn't come in to check on me. I miss Cassie, I'm still furious at Dad, Leelu will be full of nothing but excited wedding talk all morning, and now I have this unpleasant lunch to sit through, too. I don't need to write it down to know this will be a terrible day.

From downstairs Maritza exclaims in surprise, and Leelu laughs. It makes me mad that Leelu isn't upset too, but of course she isn't.

I sit up and push my covers back anyway, remembering the conversation Mom and I had about anger. My time with Leelu (before Jennifer moves in) is limited now. And if it's going to be any good, like Mom said, I have to be intentional about it. Focus on the positive. Besides, getting absorbed in one of Leelu's genius make-believe games might also help me forget this wedding for a while, the way planning Reverse Spirit Week helped me forget Cassie, at least through a weekend.

When I finish dressing and head downstairs, I'm relieved to see Maritza and Leelu have every single one of Leelu's Legos out on our giant shiny dining room table, working on a construction. It is *exactly* what I need.

"I wanted to wake you up, but Maritza says I couldn't. We've been waiting all this time!" Leelu spreads her arms wide to present her work-in-progress. "It's called Queen Liliuokalani's Millennium Falcon Taylor Swift Concert Hall and Corn Dog Stand."

I smile a little. At least she isn't calling it the Crystal

Palace of Jennifer Is Going to Be My Mom. Yet.

I join them at the table and suggest we add a rooftop pool for it, which we then spend the next hour constructing. The happy sound of Leelu's humming mixed with the calming zen of making something together does help time and everything else drop away, as I hoped. Once Dad picks me up, Queen Liliuokalani's Concert Hall has long been sailed through the grounds outside before being parked in Leelu's room, where her various dolls and stuffed animals start lining up for corn dogs. We've also created a Cupcake-O-Matic, using every one of Leelu's gears and pulleys in a single invention, and a Cyborg Regeneration Palace, too. Neither of us mentions what happened last night at dinner, and I'm so cheered up, I almost forget why Dad's taking me to lunch.

"Seems you took my text to heart," he says when we're alone in the car. "I'm glad. Does it mean you're able to talk to me now?"

A defensive hot flush rushes over me. "Talk to you about what?"

"About your unhappiness around this marriage. Or my relationship with Jennifer to begin with."

His bluntness is uncomfortable.

"I haven't said that." I'm not ready for this. Blocking out

thoughts of Dad and Jennifer all morning has kept me from preparing any good answers.

"I know you haven't. It's why I wanted us to do this today." He looks away from the road at me just long enough to make it feel unsafe. "Why I was glad we went shopping last weekend. It was my intention to discuss your feelings then, but something was going on with that friend of yours. I didn't want to press, since it was clear you were so tense, and besides we were having such a good time."

I'm shocked Dad noticed anything that day.

"You didn't want to talk then," he goes on, "and I suppose it's okay if you don't want to now. I need to tell you, however, that I see that you're unhappy, and that does matter to me."

Words finally come to the surface. "But it won't make a difference, Dad. You've said so a hundred times yourself; you and Mom are grown-ups, and I just have to go along with your decisions. You're going to do this anyway no matter how I feel about it."

Dad maneuvers us to the curb of the restaurant to park. "Perhaps it won't change anything in the grand scheme of upcoming events, you're right. But that doesn't mean I don't care."

We get out, and Dad gives his keys to the valet. I follow

him across the wide driveway, up the porch, then into the quiet, open-air dining room: a place more for business people than kids and their dads.

"Fiona," he says, quiet, when we have our seats.

I take a long drink of water so the glass can block my face.

Dad watches me glug it down. "I want to know how you really feel about this."

I stop drinking, so I don't choke. "No, you don't."

"And you know this how?" His voice is angrier. "Have you tried?"

It makes me angry, too. "Of course I've tried. I told you I didn't want to go to Disneyland with Jennifer, because it'd be her and Leelu paired up all the time instead of the three of us the way it's supposed to. I told you I don't like how she buys us all those gifts as though that will help us like her better, or how whenever you're not working you always want us to be with her. Like the park. Or dinner out all the time. We never get to have special time with you anymore, Dad. And now I don't have it with Leelu either, because Jennifer's always buddying up with her. But you're marrying her so obviously you really *don't* care what I think."

I haven't been able to look at him the whole time I say all this.

"How could I have the chance to show you," he says, waving the waiter away to buy us more time, "when this is the first I'm hearing your feelings?"

I look at him.

He looks at me.

"Really." He shakes his head in astonishment. "I had no idea."

"I have told you," I insist.

"You may have told someone else, but you didn't tell me."

To my surprise, I realize he's right. I've told my diary instead, if anyone.

"Fiona, my blossom," Dad goes on, "how am I supposed to understand what you need, when you aren't honest with me about what that might be?" His powerful lawyer voice is gone. Instead he just sounds sad. "I know these changes in our family have been difficult. I understand that you're upset with me and my decisions, but I'll only continue to frustrate and disappoint you if you don't talk to me."

He looks over his menu, giving me space to process what he just said. While I run my eyes over the list of dishes without really seeing them, something about this feels like a conversation I've had before—or, rather, one I need to have.

"I've a very loose idea of how you are," Dad picks up again when the waiter leaves with our order, "and what's happening in your life, but these are matters I hear about mainly through your mother. For example, I didn't know about Cassie until she explained to me why you were so upset about Disneyland. I would prefer to learn these issues from you, though. You're getting so grown-up, and I know things are moving fast in your world: with your friends, your interests, maybe a little romantically with boys. Or, I guess, girls. Whatever the case, I don't want to miss out on who you're becoming, just because you're holding in your anger with me. I'd appreciate a chance to listen to your feelings, and share my own side. Maybe we'll both learn something, and benefit. I would like that. But I asked you to this lunch because I need your help. I can't accomplish this by myself; I could use you meeting me at least halfway."

Having Dad talk to me in such a grown-up way feels strange and a little scary. At first I'm not sure I know how to respond on the same level, until I think of Aja telling me that friends say things straight. Remember leaping into new experiences, even when I was scared.

Maybe there's a lot more I can revise besides my writing and my wardrobe, even if it takes several tries. Even if I still don't know the ending.

I take a sip of water, and then look Dad in the eye. "Okay."

• • •

We spend almost two hours talking. At first it's hard to explain to Dad all the ways in which I don't like Jennifer, and sometimes he argues with my statements, but he does listen. He's surprised when I say all the gifts are excessive, and I'm surprised when he agrees that father/daughter time is important to keep. He confesses how badly he felt when I didn't come along on vacation, and that he should have fought harder to make that work. I tell him how much I gained from creative writing camp, and how I've managed to create good things out of the bad ones that have happened. How brave I've felt getting through the most terrible moments. It doesn't change the fact that he and Jennifer are still getting married, or that I'm not happy about it, but in the course of our conversation, something between us shifts in a better direction.

As we wait for the car, Dad puts a hand on my shoulder. "I'm sorry," he says. "That we had to fight before you could come to me. You're right, I haven't paid attention, and your mother was right that I should have spoken to you and your sister about the engagement privately first. I wanted what I wanted, and thought what I thought, I guess. Sometimes I still expect Mom to speak out of anger instead of sense. But that's unfair to who she is now, and it was unfair to you."

I nod, a tightness prickling in my throat and my eyes. Dad isn't the type to apologize to people much, so hearing it feels strange, even if it's what I've been waiting for all lunch without knowing it. That he understands Mom so well, and talked to her about this first, feels important, too. None of it magically fixes everything, but it has made a difference. Maybe not in ways I'd expected, but deep down, I still feel a knot inside me has loosened: one I wasn't aware was there before.

And I can think of someone else I might feel better talking to, too.

Chapter Nineteen

I don't think Mom will call me back immediately, since she's busy with her importers in San Francisco, but after I message her she FaceTimes me right away.

"Are you all right?" she wants to know.

I assure her yes. "Dad and I had lunch today. We talked. About a lot of things."

Mom's face relaxes. "I know he's been wanting to have a conversation with you."

"Yeah, we did, but it made me realize I've needed to have one with you too. For a long time, I think. I just haven't exactly known how."

"Well, I'm eager to listen, blossom."

I spill the more recent dilemma with Aja first, since

we've at least discussed that together a little, but eventually I get to the important stuff about Cassie, and my diary, and why seeing Kendra in the library was so upsetting. I tell her about dumping soda on Kendra, seeing Cheyenne at the thrift store, and missing Cassie even though I'm still angry about what happened. Wishing at least Cassie could know about it. That I wanted her with me, Sanders, and Evie at Teamer Park, too.

"That's a lot." Mom looks a little overwhelmed. "I'm surprised you've had so much going on that you haven't been able to tell me about."

I feel another guilty twinge, like I did with Dad. "It never seemed like the right time. And I didn't think—"

"You can tell me anything, Fiona. I hope you know that."

"Really, I was afraid you'd call Cassie's mom. That you'd try to help but only make it worse."

Her nod is thoughtful. "Well, to be honest, Serena and I have spoken a little about you two not seeing each other. I don't think either of us knew the scope, though."

"I'm sorry."

"You've been processing it on your own." She means my diary.

But I know what she'll say next. What I want to say, too. "Talking to people out loud might help even more."

"I just never want you to feel you have to hide."

I assure her I don't anymore. That it's better now.

"Is there anything else you need to tell me?" she makes sure.

I consider. "I don't like Jennifer. Or"—I think more clearly—"I don't like her around all the time, and that when she is, it's like I lose Leelu to her."

Mom chuckles in empathy. "That girl worships you. But if you're scared of someone else coming between you—whomever it is—you're the only one who can keep it from happening."

I'm not sure how I can keep Jennifer and Leelu from fusing together, but I thank Mom for the good talk.

"Oh, thank *you*," she says. "I'm so sorry you felt you had to struggle on your own."

It hits me, clear: "Maybe I needed to."

We trade *I love you*s, and Mom says we can talk more when she's back.

Without too much thought after we hang up, I knock on the wall that separates my room and Leelu's: "Hey, sissie?"

She knocks back, two times, which means I can come in. She's propped up on a stack of turquoise and pink pillows in her pajamas, reading a book she found at our last trip to the library.

"You know our list?" I ask.

"Yeah. We're almost finished. There's only, like, four things left."

"I know. So I was wondering if, before school starts, we could go back and revisit the most fun things."

Her dimples pop out. "You mean like Legos?"

I'm glad this morning is already considered a highlight for her. "Sure, that. But I was thinking, tomorrow night, just you and me, maybe roller-skating?"

She nearly trips out of the bed to grab me in a hug, and then runs down the hall, calling for Dad. He's clearly in an extra-big Please the Daughters mood, because he drops us off together at the rink the next night, without even insisting on staying himself. Nobody in my grade really skates anymore—it's for littler kids, or else the big ones in college—but Leelu loves the lights and the music, and unlike me, she's fearless on her skates. A lot of the time she zips around between other skaters, lapping me over and over, though at slow songs we clasp hands while she skates backward and I skate forward.

We're doing this during one of the first slow skates when I decide to ask her.

"Hey, Leelu?"

"Yeah?"

"We haven't talked yet about Dad and Jennifer's announcement."

She makes a confused face.

So I ask straight out. "What do you think about Jennifer, really?"

"She's pretty. And, she's fun."

"Fun because she always buys you presents and does whatever you want?"

"No. Fun because she plays with me. Better than Dad anyway."

"I play with you."

"You're the best player, but now you're always busy with your writing or your friends. Like when we were at the park and you just left me behind to jump off that big cliff. You didn't even want to go on vacation with me."

Since I'm steering, I am afraid to look fully down at her, but I don't need to see those big brown eyes to feel her sadness.

"You're always so excited when she's around, though," I say. "And you were having so much fun in all those Disneyland pictures—sharing your own suite—I didn't think you missed me at all. I thought you liked it better with her. Every time she's around, you're jumping up and down."

"Disneyland was fun," she agrees. "But it would've been way funner with you there. We had to split up on a lot of the rides. If you had been with me, we could have ridden together and they could be in another car. Plus, Dad's no good at I spy in line. He always has to check his phone or something. And Jennifer does it too easy. They were holding hands and kissing a lot too—I didn't have a pair to be in."

I'd been so worried about being left out of the Jennifer-Leelu partnership, I didn't consider that, without me there, something similar would happen to Leelu. If she felt left out or like a third wheel, it's my fault.

I remember Dad's apology to me, and how good it felt.

"I'm sorry I did that to you, Loodeeloo. I wasn't thinking about how it would seem from your side."

She nods, but she's still sad. We skate together in quiet, under the blue and red lights, the spinning of the multiple tiny disco balls on the ceiling. I'm not sure what I can say to her next.

"You don't like Jennifer." She's not asking me, she's saying it.

"I don't . . ." *Like how she gets in our business all the time*, I think, but that's not the real truth: the deep one inside me being covered by the other story I'm telling myself. "I don't like that our family got broken up, or that Mommy has to live in the condo and we have to live in Dad's new place instead of our big house, all together. I don't like it that Dad wants to be married to someone else."

Leelu nods again. The slow set ends, and the white

lights go back up. Couples around us separate, and kids Leelu's age start chasing each other around the rink again. Leelu turns to skate forward too, but she doesn't let go of my hand.

"Do you think Jennifer will have a baby?" she asks, timid.

I nearly laugh and stop skating, it surprises me so much, but when Leelu looks up at me, I can see how distressed she is.

"Have you been worried about that?"

She bites her lip. "Uh-huh."

I guess I'm not the only one who hasn't been saying things. I skate a few strides, trying to think how *I* would feel about a baby. If they had one right now, I'd be graduating high school when it started kindergarten. I would hardly know it at all. I'd still be the biggest sister, though. Leelu would have to give up being the baby herself.

"I don't know if Jennifer or Dad want a baby. But if they do, I don't think they're going to have one any time soon." I didn't think they'd be getting *married* so soon, either, but I don't need to worry Leelu more. "If they do, Daddy will be there to talk to you about it, I promise. Even though he works a lot, he really does care what we think."

I see her not exactly believing me, but she'll find out, the way I did, when she needs to. Before this week, nobody could have told me I'd have a conversation like the one I did with Dad yesterday, either.

"And besides"—I wiggle my wrist, making our hands flop between us—"if they do, that baby will have a big sister like you, which means it will be very, very lucky."

"You're teasing."

"No, I'm serious." I let go and put my hands on my hips, sassy. "I'll be too busy with my writing and my friends, as you say. Who else will teach it all the best movies and songs, or how to play Rescue Mermaid, and the rules for TVD?"

She giggles at this. "Yeah, you'll be too big then. All you'll care about is your phone. And kissing."

"That's right. Don't forget checking my skin for pimples, either."

"Ew! Or armpit hair!" she squeals.

I fire back, "Horror movies and surfing," and our conversation derails into all the gross and dumb things teenagers do, which is only interrupted by an old Taylor Swift song we love but haven't heard in a long time. We swing our hips and mouth all the words as we skate, not caring what anyone around us may think. Round and round we go together the rest of the night, until we're sweaty, tired, and leaning on each other in the backseat of Dad's car, where I feel, for the first time in a while, that my sister and I do have something that no one else can destroy, after all. Not even a wicked (or just super-enthusiastic) stepmother.

It's not until we're home and getting ready for bed that I remember the world outside my family, and think to check my phone.

Hi Fiona! Evie wrote while Leelu and I were skating. **Do you know about the party tomorrow?**

Just got this—what party? I type back.

She answers fast, even though it's late: **I hope it's okay but I talked to Aja. She wants you to come, and said she'd invite you herself, but I guess she's too embarrassed to ask. She said she'd tell Tyrick not to be there if you don't want him to come. She feels bad.**

I consider this. I suppose I'll need to get used to Evie telling other people things even if I'm not ready for her to yet, but I'm not mad. It's just hard to picture what it might be like, seeing Aja or Tyrick, after so much time. And everything in between.

What kind of party is it?

A pool party.

Who's coming?

She's inviting a lot of girls from chorus. Some boys too. River's friends. It should be fun.

Do you think I could bring Sanders? I tentatively send.

It's probably too late to ask him, and it might be weird for me to bring someone to Aja's party whom she doesn't know, but having both Evie and Sanders there will make sure I have a good time, no matter what happens.

I will tell her to let you! He's so fun!

There really isn't time to think about any of it, since Sanders and Dad say yes right away when I ask the next morning, and the party starts at eleven. There's barely a moment to even consider what I'm wearing before Evie, and then Sanders, is ringing our doorbell, chatting and laughing in the living room like there was never any awkwardness between them. I'm glad, for more than one reason than that it helps distract me from my nervousness about seeing Aja.

When we arrive at Aja's house, Evie leads us straight across the street to the neighborhood pool, where there's music, kids laughing and splashing in the water, and a grill full of hot dogs and hamburgers. She introduces us to Aja's dad, and points out a bunch of other girls we know. Seeing them makes me excited to be back in chorus again, and as I wave and say hi, I notice several other kids I wasn't aware Aja was friends with. I say so to Evie.

"Kendra's not the only one who can have a big party this weekend." She raises her eyebrow in a grown-up way.

"Lots of people are here just because of that."

The unexpected mention of my redheaded nemesis pulls Cassie back to the front of my mind. Is she at Kendra's today too? Does she know they were making fun of her at the mall? Or is she siting there sipping fizzy punch and tugging her swimsuit top, having no idea how they really feel? Does she still even like Cory, or has that changed for her, the way my feelings for Tyrick have? What would we tell each other, if we somehow were able to talk about these parties later? Do we still have anything in common, or is everything just too different now?

My trance is broken when I see Aja with River and a few other kids over by the grill, laughing at something River's friend is saying. Tyrick isn't with them, so probably he's not even here, which is a relief but a little disappointing. Aja glances up in a giggle, and our eyes meet. She's surprised to see me, but glad, and shy, and something else. Maybe sorry. I have the feeling all those same expressions are happening on my face, too, so I lift my hand in a wave, but a girl walks in front of me with a plate of food, and in that brief second, Aja's attention shifts back to the kids she's with. Somehow, though, it doesn't bother me. Maybe we don't need a big makeup with lots of hugging and tears. Maybe we can have had our disagreements, and still be friends anyway. We can keep revising our friendship until we find something that works for both of us.

"Should we eat first?" Evie asks.

"Or get in the pool," Sanders says, like that's the real answer.

They look to me to make the final vote, but I can't say anything, because there's Tyrick, coming straight over.

"Hey, Fiona."

I'm so surprised. Not only to see him, but that he walked right up.

"Hey," I say.

"How's your summer been?" He kicks one foot against the other, unable to look me in the eye. I feel suddenly glad I wore my one-piece instead of my tankini. It would make me even more self-conscious than I am right now.

"Good?" It's true now, but it also hasn't been, and I have no idea how much of that I could explain to him.

"Yeah."

He still can't look at me. I remember liking him so much, and then not liking him, and now feeling unsure what to think about him at all. I'm wishing I could back out of this conversation without making either of us feel worse, when a hand stretches around my side to shake with Tyrick.

"I'm Sanders," he says, stepping closer. "You a writer too?"

Tyrick seems baffled by Sanders's friendly directness.

He's also eyeing him like he's trying to tell if Sanders is my date or not. But Sanders jumps straight into the conversation as easily as he does with everyone else, explaining to Tyrick how we met in writing camp, and all the stories we wrote. Evie chimes in next about our jump off Teamer Cliff, and that Sanders inspired us, which makes Tyrick's eyes go wide in an impressed way. Before long our whole conversation flows from daredevil acts to the most terrifying roller coaster we've ever been on, and then what we'll do after the robot takeover.

Finally we get into the pool, but not long after Sanders gets hungry, so since he's my guest I join him to scarf down a couple of hot dogs. Evie's still in the water, crammed inside a giant inner tube with four other girls, all of them singing Beyoncé. They're sticking to the shallow end so they don't get jumped on by the kids taking running leaps off the diving board, including Tyrick.

"Tyrick is cool," Sanders says, watching him.

"You think so?"

"Sure." Sanders shrugs. "Not as cool as you, but still."

We trade smiles. Talking things out has been a theme for me lately, but I know there's no need to tell Sanders the whole uncomfortable arc with Tyrick. Especially not that I used to write down every single thing he said in English class.

"And he likes you." Sanders looks at me, sly.

I flush. It's embarrassing that Sanders noticed, but somehow pleasing too. So does that mean I want Tyrick to still like me? Is there a way I could ever like him again?

"Come on." Sanders puts his empty plate down on the nearby table. "This party needs some ninjas."

He makes a sudden lunge for the edge of the pool, leaping into the air at the last minute and screaming an ancient Japanese curse. He manages not to land on anyone, but the giant splash he creates cascades over a dozen different kids, including Evie and her inner-tube girls. At first it seems they might be mad about it, but within moments, the pool is full of the most legendary splash war ever. The second I slip into the shallow end with Evie, there's so much water flying around I'm immediately soaked by people I can barely see. So I get into it too. We thrash and thrash at each other, choking and laughing, not caring who we're aiming at. Someone hits my arm. I feel my legs kicking against another person. It's a giant free-for-all, and no one cares who likes who, or who knows who else—only that we're having fun. A lot of it.

Eventually the splashing dies down, and somebody calls for a game of survivor. As kids argue over who gets to be shark and who's submarine, I catch Tyrick looking my way from the other side of the pool. I smile, and roll my eyes to show I think the fighting's silly. He smiles back. But then Aja yells, "Go," and there's nothing but the game, until the shadows start getting a little longer, and parents appear in Aja's curved driveway across the street.

"Bye, Fiona," Tyrick calls as he's leaving with River and two other boys.

I wave, and Evie elbows me, but I swallow the smile that wants to bloom up, because I'm still not sure about him.

Above us, Aja's standing at the top of the stairs like a queen, wrapped in a towel and thanking everyone for coming as they leave. Looking at her standing there so tall and regal and happy, I feel like giving her a small hug before I go.

"It was nice of you to invite me," I say when I get up the steps.

Beads of water are glimmering in her dark twists. "I'm glad you were here."

There's more to say—that I'm genuinely glad she's with River, and that it was nice for her to be so invested in me and Tyrick at first. Maybe also I want to say I'm sorry, though I'm not sure about what exactly. But I lose my chance to say anything, because two other girls come up to thank her for the party too. From the look we exchanged when I first got here, and how she's being now, though, I can tell she understands.

I slip away from Aja behind the other girls and head to the sidewalk where Evie and Sanders are waiting. I know as good as it is to talk things out with people, sometimes it's just as good to let them pass: to accept that things are different, without saying anything at all, in your diary or anywhere else.

What if, I write before bed since I can't stop thinking it, *I had been able to say any of those negative things to you, before? Would it have made a difference, hearing them from me instead of her? Would we have survived?*

Getting back into the groove with Evie and Aja crams my mind and my feed with messages and photos, pushing out any lingering thoughts I might still be having of Cassie. Evie invites us to a slumber party at her house, and Aja suggests we do horseback riding on the beach before school starts. Plus one more round of back-to-school shopping, and a return to Room for Dessert. It reminds me that I want to see some of my writing camp friends before summer ends, so I suggest a big group movie outing. I ask Leelu to help us pick which film, so that we can take her along, too.

When we're back at Mom's Monday, right away she says I look like a changed person.

"You weren't in San Francisco *that* long," I say.

"But you were one unhappy little flower last time I saw you."

I agree, but assure her things are different. I sit at the little counter between our living room and the kitchen, and while she puts together dinner, I tell her all about Aja's party—including the parts about Tyrick. Mom listens, asks questions, and offers guidance in the same way she has before, but it feels like she's listening more too. Like Dad was.

When I move to fetch plates from the cabinet and set the table, Mom reaches out and takes my chin in her hand.

"You're such a lovely, grown-up girl. Do you know that?"

I remember Dad saying something similar. And feeling it myself, at Aja's pool party.

I nod.

"And I'm very proud of you."

She hugs me tight, her fierce strength holding me close. But for the first time I can feel strength pulsing out from me, too.

Mom loosens our hold. "Your sister should help with the silverware, don't you think?"

I smile and skip down the hall to stick my head in our room.

"Leelu, time to set the table."

She doesn't look up from the game she's playing. "Let me finish this. And your phone was ringing."

I tell her dinner's mostly ready, but I also take a second to quickly check my screen. I figure it's Evie making official plans for the coming weekend, but when I look under missed calls, there's Cassie's picture, smiling at me.

I haven't seen this photo in so long, it seems like a trick. I took it of her last fall, when we went apple picking with her family—a trip Cassie suggested, because it was around the time Dad bought his new house, and she hoped it would cheer me up. She's sitting high in one of the trees, surrounded by leaves and yellow-skinned apples. The sun is glinting in her eyes and in her hair. She looks pretty, and happy, and best of all, relaxed.

Staring at the golden image, I think, *I don't know this girl anymore.*

And also, *I miss her.*

"Girls, it's time," Mom calls from the hallway, close to impatient.

I decide to wait until after dinner to figure out what to do about Cassie. Partly because I don't know what to say to her, but also because Mom really doesn't like postponing our dinner schedule. Even Leelu hops off the bed and rushes out. When we've finished cleaning up from dinner, though, and she and Leelu are settling in together on the couch, I excuse myself to my room.

"What are you up to?" Mom wants to know.

I consider not telling her. Not because I'm hiding, or even because I think she'd jump into advising mode, but because I'm honestly not positive what I'll do next. I just want to look at that picture again, see if I feel the same way.

"Cassie called me," I confess.

Mom's surprised, too. "And?"

"And I was thinking of calling her back."

"Do you need to talk about it?" The warm understanding in her eyes says more than she needs to with words.

"I think I'm okay right now," I tell her.

Mom turns her attention back to Leelu and the remote. "Well, you know where to find me if you need me. If you speak with her, I hope it goes well."

Saying out loud that I'm talking to Cassie still doesn't help me understand what will happen when I do. To stall, I open my old diary, and then the butterfly journal I've been writing in since camp, flipping through entries in both and looking for inspiration. I read over my whole summer, remembering my agony and laughing a little about it, too. There are angry thoughts, and sad ones. Happy ones, as well. Parts where I sound like I don't know if I can be friends again with Cassie, and some where I hope I will. So much isn't cut-and-dry, only frustrating because nothing is clear. I turn another page, to the entry about the cliff, when I wrote about Evie: *she's changed and I'm changed but we're still together, the same friends but both of us somehow different.*

When Cassie answers, she sounds as nervous as I feel. "Fiona?"

"Hi. I saw you called."

"I didn't want to just leave a voice mail."

"We were having dinner."

"Oh." There's a pause. "How are you?" she asks.

I still don't trust her, so I don't know how to answer this honestly.

"I'm fine. What about you?"

"We're in Maine."

I try to picture it. "Maine?" Mom said Cassie had gone on a trip, but I had no idea she was going *that* far.

"Yeah, it's a long story, but my vacation with Nono and Grandpa Howe got a little—redirected."

"Oh."

We're both quiet. Maybe she's remembering, like I am, that I don't know anything about her grandparents' wedding, let alone this honeymoon. Or why she's suddenly calling him "Grandpa."

"My cousin's here," she says. "Lana."

"Yeah?"

"You would like her. She's really—well, anyway. She reminds me of you."

I wait, feeling a bunch of mixed things moving too fast to identify.

"She's the one who suggested I call."

When I still don't say anything, she makes a sighing noise—more sad than annoyed.

"Could we see each other?" she asks.

"Okay," I say. Even though I'm not sure what that would be like. I try to picture inviting her over, going to Room for Dessert and splitting a cookie-dough brownie, or any of the other things we used to do together. It's hard to imagine us there now. While some of this conversation feels a little like old times, I know we can't immediately go back to the same activities, the same closeness we had. At least, not right away.

"Maybe we should go skating," I say.

"On the boardwalk?" There's a little of the old Cassie disapproval in her voice.

"No, I mean at the rink."

"Does anybody go there? I don't think it's still open."

"Leelu loves it. We went the other night."

"How is ol' Loodeeloo?"

"She's good. We've been spending more time together, which I'm glad about since—you know. Since school's starting again soon." I'd been about to say "since Jennifer will be around all the time now," until I remembered Cassie doesn't know about the engagement. Or Disneyland, even.

"Well, if Leelu's into it, I guess it's all right," she says. "And at least we know we won't run into Kendra Mack."

When we both laugh, I discover I actually like the sound of it: our voices carefully merging, even if only for a few seconds, back together.

Chapter Twenty

The night Cassie and I are supposed to go skating, I'm nervous. We haven't talked since her phone call, but she has shared some photos during their long drive back from Maine. The super-friendly ones of her and Lana surprise me, at first, and for a second I wonder if Kendra and I have simply been replaced by this thick-haired girl with her happy, open smile, but the more I examine them (and tell Mom my concerns), the more I think Lana looks like someone I might want to know myself. I definitely admire the checkered cap she has on in some of the pictures, anyway. And if Cassie has a new best friend whom I actually *like* this time, maybe that won't be so bad. After all, if we find a way to make up, I'll want her to be friends with Evie, and Sanders, too.

Part of what makes me nervous, though, is understanding that just because Cassie and I are meeting up, it doesn't mean things are going back to the old way they were. Even from our stilted phone call, I can tell from Cassie's voice that she's not the same. And she knows I'm not, either. When we finally really talk, there may be things that don't fit anymore—things we'll have to share with other friends instead.

But what if the new me and the new her won't go together at all? Even if we're willing to revise a hundred times, what if we can't turn this into a story that has a good ending?

To calm myself down on the way over, I lean across to show Leelu the latest pictures of me, Evie, and Aja. I remind myself that Aja and I had our own kind of break, and we're okay now, even if we're both different.

I just hope there's enough left of the old Cassie, and the old Fiona, to help tie the new parts together.

Cassie's not there yet when we arrive, but I pay for our admission so Leelu can go straight to joining her friends. The skating rink is more crowded than it was the last time we were here, and to my surprise there are even some kids

I recognize from school. As Leelu changes into her skates, I watch for Cassie. I wonder if she'll look different. What she'll be wearing. It took me forever to choose an outfit from the new stuff I've gotten over the summer, and I'm still not sure about these yellow leggings or the T-shirt dress I got at Plato's Closet covered in lemons and tangerines. Cassie will probably think, especially with the red beret, that it's all too noisy, but I'm telling myself it's a good combo of the old and the new. If she says something snarky it will just be a sign.

A couple of minutes later I see her walking up to the entrance, and am surprisingly relieved she looks a lot the same. At least, her hair and clothes do—sophisticated and stylish as always, especially with those long beaded earrings. But her face seems less harsh, and definitely less confident, even though she's wearing a little makeup. The windows facing the parking lot are mirrored on the outside, so I watch her undetected. Walking up, she definitely doesn't look like the jaunty, cocky girl who made fun of me for dressing up like a princess during Spirit Week.

"Hey, Cassie," I call as soon as she's through the glass door.

She flinches at the sound of her name, but smiles in relief when she sees me waving.

"I waited to get my skates," I say.

"I don't know if I remember how to put them on."

"I'll make Leelu show you if you can't," I tease her, automatic. "But probably it's like riding a bike."

Cassie looks out at the kids already skating. "Where is she, anyway? I thought she'd come say hi to me."

"With her little girlfriends." I look with Cassie for my sister's peachy shirt in the crowd of kids on the rink floor, but instead of finding her, I see someone else I recognize.

"Oh no" comes out of my mouth before I can stop myself.

"What?"

"I don't know if you want to know."

She shrinks and grips my arm instinctively.

"No, it's not any of them," I assure her, both of us knowing exactly who.

"Who then?"

But I don't have to say, because Cory skates right in front of us alongside his friend Jeannette.

Cassie's face is a mix of things: horror, and delight. Uncertainty, too. Maybe jealousy, though I don't know her real feelings about him anymore. Or if she ever found out about that awful joke Kendra and Izzy were playing on her, whatever it was.

"So should we?" I indicate the rink.

Cassie's eyes are still worried. "Maybe we should get some fries or something?"

I say okay, and we clomp together to the neon-lit snack bar, with its checkerboard floor and groovy pleather booths. When Cassie orders her Sprite, I can't help smiling.

She catches my expression. "What?"

"Oh, I—I don't know." It's not what I should start with: how I soaked Kendra in the mall. Not yet, anyway. "Why don't you want to see Cory?"

I can tell she's blushing, even with blue light glowing off her cheeks. "It's a long story."

I shrug. "I can listen."

So we sit in a curvy little booth, sharing sweet potato fries, and then a basket of tempura green beans, relaying snippets of summer. Cassie tells me the horror story of Izzy's brother's phone, and how Kendra used it to send her messages she thought were from Cory. I tell her about seeing Cheyenne at the thrift store, and how nice she was to me, which then leads to my describing—without shyness or hesitation—the interesting changes in my wardrobe. Cassie actually seems curious, and narrates an afternoon when she, Lana, and their grandparents went to an art festival, and purposefully picked out the strangest pieces as potential Christmas presents for each other. After that I describe the water war at Aja's party, and plummeting from

Teamer Cliff, which means then I backtrack into the long story of writing camp, and who Sanders is.

"Oh—" I interrupt myself halfway, because now that we're talking more easily, there is one big thing she should finally know. "Get this: Dad and Jennifer are getting married."

Cassie's brown-black eyes at first go wide, but then her whole face scrunches in concern. "Oh, Fiona. That's terrible."

It sends a pang pulsing through my rib cage. Dad and Jennifer's engagement is the one thing that I still can't make into something good yet, and I know it may be a while before I do. Cassie's sympathetic face now reminds me just how much I could've used this side of her—the listening side—more than once this summer.

"I should apologize," she says, serious.

It's so sudden, I'm not sure how to look at her, quite.

"For turning my back on you," she goes on. "I did it, I guess, because I was mad." She picks at the uneaten shards of our sweet potato fries, but doesn't eat any. "And hurt by what you wrote about me. In, you know, your diary."

We're still not looking at each other, but I nod.

"Maybe a little curious too," she goes on, "to see what it was like, being in their group. But . . . I should have talked to you."

It's surreal, hearing all this. How familiar it sounds.

"I should have talked to you, too," I feel brave enough to say. There's no hesitation in my voice, but the gap of her silent surprise gives me even more courage. "I wasn't always honest with you, and it probably felt awful, hearing my inner thoughts from somebody like Kendra, instead of me. Especially when I was so mean sometimes. The things I said in there, they weren't true, exactly." After all this time, I still don't know what Cassie heard, or how she feels about it now, but I know she deserves an apology. "Or, at least, they weren't the whole truth. I just thought—I don't even know what I thought. I guess I didn't believe you'd listen if I didn't always agree with you. That you'd get mad, or it would mean something about our friendship. Which wasn't fair to you, and made things come out worse than they were. I don't know, really."

After a second, she clears her throat. "You're right, I probably would've gotten mad. At least a little. Lana says I have a bad temper."

"You just feel things and take action, that's all."

"Yeah, but maybe I should think about things more sometimes." She's quiet a moment. "I've been doing a lot of thinking, actually. And one thing I think is that we have a lot to talk about."

"I know we do," I agree.

"One thing I missed?" she says.

I still can't meet her eyes. "Yeah?"

"Never being able to admit it when things were bad."

I shake my head to show I'm not sure what she means.

"With Kendra . . ." She stares at the skaters moving under the blurry green lights beyond us. "I had to pretend I was okay with everything, even when I hated it. Gates Morrill and Billy Keegan, for example? They did the most revolting things at lunch. Stuffing hamburgers and french fries into their milk shakes. Salsa. And then drinking it. It was disgusting."

I remember.

"But everyone'd be egging them on. One time Neftali poured half her kale smoothie in there. Kendra gave Billy a piece of her sushi roll. And there were other things, not just at lunch. It was like this whole complicated game of pretend, all the time. With everyone. So much I didn't know—almost everything, I guess."

The sadness in her voice allows me to finally look at her.

"Lana showed me that," she finishes in explanation. "And Nono, too. Though, of course, finding out that Cory wasn't really texting me helped."

"Do you still like him?" I venture.

She glances again at the skaters. "I don't know. I don't know if it's him I like, or—"

I understand before she says it. "If you liked liking him."

We smile at each other. Now would be a good time, maybe, to tell her about Tyrick, and then my fight with Aja, or my heart-to-heart with Dad—so many things. We've covered a lot, sitting here, and aside from a few hesitations and pauses, it's felt surprisingly natural. But there's so much she still doesn't know—so many parts we haven't even touched on, the least of which being how she ended up in Maine. Trying to span this giant distance we let grow between us feels daunting.

She smiles at me again, this time shy, but it's enough to let me know—or, at least, hope—that eventually, with work, we will bridge this new awkward gap.

Over our heads, an old Lenny Kravitz song squalls out, breaking the moment.

"Lana loves this song," she says. "Mind if I tell her it's playing?"

"Go ahead."

While she texts her cousin, I look for Leelu again. This time she's easy to spot—skating backward while holding hands with one of her friends. I watch carefully, too, for Cory and Jeannette, though after three full rounds I still don't see them. Maybe they left. Maybe, when school starts, we'll somehow find out they really are dating now.

Or maybe we won't care anymore, since they'll be in high school and we'll be on to something else. Something new to watch, together.

"We should go out there," I say, but Cassie's frowning at her phone when I turn back. "Everything okay?"

"Oh. Yes, it's actually fine. Great, really."

I quirk my eyebrows, wanting to know more. Not just about Lana, but about who Cassie is in this new friendship, too.

"Long story. Let's at least skate a couple rounds. Don't want to waste the rental fee."

We parse our way carefully across the carpeted floor, Cassie watching both the skaters zipping by us—probably looking for Cory—and the floor in front of her, so she doesn't fall on her butt. Eventually we make it to the edge and step gingerly out onto the slick glossy rink.

"I don't know." Cassie grabs my arm for balance as a tall boy wearing big earphones whips past.

"Come on." I reach down for her hand, in part to hold us both steady, part because it just feels right. At least for now. "It's not as scary as it looks. You have to just do it to find out."

PEOPLE TO THANK FOR HELPING ME WRITE THIS BOOK: A LIST

by Terra Elan McVoy

- Anica Rissi, because she has good ideas and I have good ideas, and yet, it is somehow even more supersparkleamazing when we put them together.
- Alexandra Arnold, because I never thought that after having the best editor in the world, I'd get the other best editor in the world. THANK YOU for all the time, encouragement, and enthusiasm, and also for pushing me.
- Meredith Kaffel Simonoff, who is not only a smart and helpful agent, but a lovely one too.
- Laurel & Elizabeth for all that ~~writing~~ talking time together.
- Every single fan of *Drive Me Crazy* who wanted more from Cassie, Lana, and Fiona's world. BUT HUGELY

MOST ESPECIALLY THANKS to Jojo Desir, Lee
Rachel Carlomogno, Nora Colussy-Estes, Emily
Becker, and Will Walton, whose encouraging faces I
pictured while writing.

- Katherine Tegen, Heather Daugherty, Ro Romanello,
  and all the delightful people at HarperCollins who
  have welcomed me with such amazing kindness,
  and were excited enough by *Drive Me Crazy* to want
  another book.
- Ida, Gavin, and Grant from Kids & Companions at
  Little Shop of Stories for helping me come up with
  Fiona's creative writing camp story ideas.
- The Bat Cave writers, for inspiration, but mostly a
  serious education.
- Every single person who has ever cheered me on,
  either in person or online. Writing is great, but it can
  also be hard to know if you are doing a good job.
  Friends who high-five me, hug me, congratulate me,
  smile at me, ask about me, listen to me, and otherwise
  help me keep going are—well, it's hard to say exactly,
  but I really couldn't do it without them.
- That guy who I'm married to, because there's none of
  this without him.

NAVIGATE

the twists and turns of friendship with

TERRA ELAN McVOY